DEAD IMAGE

D1211381

By the same author

Non-Fiction

Lady Policeman

Reluctant Nightingale

The British Policewoman: Her Story

Marlborough Street: The Story of a London Court

Tales from Bow Street

Blue Murder? Policemen Under Suspicion

Dreadful Deeds and Awful Murders: Scotland Yard's First Detective 1829–1878

Scotland Yard Casebook: The Making of the CID 1865–1935

Fiction

Dead Born

Death in Perspective

Dead Letters

Dead End

Dead Fall

Dead Loss

Dead Centre

DEAD IMAGE

A DETECTIVE SERGEANT BEST MYSTERY

Joan Lock

The
Mystery
Press

First published by Robert Hale 2000
This paperback edition first published by The Mystery Press 2012,
an imprint of

The History Press
The Mill, Brimscombe Port
Stroud, Gloucestershire, GL5 2QG
www.thehistorypress.co.uk

British Library Cataloguing in Publication Data.
A catalogue record for this book is available from the British Library.

ISBN 978 0 7524 6455 8

Typesetting and origination by The History Press
Printed in Great Britain
Manufacturing managed by Jellyfish Print Solutions Ltd

Chapter One

When it happened it was that quietest of times when the night is nearly done and most people are as removed from daily cares as they are ever likely to be.

When it happened, those nearby were catapulted from the depths of their slumber by a thunderous roar and a shudder which could be heard and felt twenty miles away. In a darkness more dense after the blinding flash which had accompanied the terrible noise, houses rocked and started to collapse around their terror-stricken and confused occupants.

Those who were able rushed, panicking, on to the streets, convinced that it must be an earthquake or even the end of the world. For some, it was.

Faces lit up at the sight of her as she hurried towards the park that early October evening in 1874, not only because she was porcelain pretty in her pale-blue ensemble, but also because of the light in her eyes and her eager step. Later, people were to remember seeing her and smiling with pleasure.

In her right hand, she held a blue and white striped parasol which served more to ward off the soft mist of autumn rain than to protect from the waning evening sun. In her left, she carried a small, plaid carpet bag.

Strictly speaking, she knew she should not have brought the bag. Strictly speaking (given the beginnings of a seasonal nip in the air) it would have been more sensible to wear her warmer, chestnut-brown ensemble. But blue made the best of her and the style was extremely becoming, with its severely straight front and froth of frills and flounces spilling out behind her as she hurried towards the canal bridge. Such an occasion demanded such a dress.

Further east down the canal, narrow-boat steerer, Charles Baxton, was wearily contemplating the stack of goods waiting to be loaded on to his craft at the City Road Wharf. *His* garb was of the style common to many of his fellow boatmen: grimy corduroy breeches, short canvas smock, neckerchief, and heavy, Blucher boots. He was far from elated by the prospect of what stretched before him that evening: the loading of sacks of sugar, currants, nuts and beans; drums of benzoline, bundles of boarding and barrels of gunpowder – making sure he got them in the right order. Heaviest things in first. Each customer's orders kept together as far as possible to aid fast unloading. Speed was essential on the fly boats.

As she neared the meeting place the girl in blue spotted the smart young man waiting for her. He was leaning on the railings of the canal's most handsome bridge, his head down, watching idly as a black-and-white-liveried boat glided beneath him. He seemed to be frowning. Did he think she wasn't coming? She called out to him but her breathless voice failed to carry.

Why did he look so serious? Had something gone wrong? Not just serious, she realized as she came closer, but also intense – almost angry in fact. In fact, when he finally turned around, he looked quite ferocious. Then his expression softened rapidly into a welcoming smile. Was that just how he looked when deep in thought, she wondered? Or had he really been angry? They had a lot to learn about each other. She smiled back and ran towards him joyfully.

It was ten minutes past nine at the still-bustling, gas-lit quayside. Baxton and company load checker Joseph Minchin were surveying the now fully loaded *Tilbury* with some satisfaction. It did sit rather low in the water, that was true – hardly surprising given its twenty-ton cargo. But it was all clothed-up with a spanking new tarpaulin and ready to go at last. They were not to know that all their efforts were to be in vain. Nor that their toil would later be picked over and analysed by men who had not done a day's physical work in their lives.

It was raining lightly when, just before midnight, Baxton's boat slipped out of the City Road basin, turned left into the Regent's Canal and entered the first of the five locks he had to negotiate before they came to the long and peaceful stretch of canal which wandered through Regent's Park. Then he would be able to get tucked up for a while.

Once through that first lock, the *Tilbury* became one of a chain of five fly boats hooked together – to be pulled along by the *Ready*, a busy little steamtug already puffing away and lighting up the darkness with its firefly-spray of sparks. Baxton's boat was the central bead in this mobile necklace, and his chief task was to prevent his craft from colliding either with the canalside bank or the other boats in the chain. Not easy in the dark.

The darkness also robbed the work of one of its few compensations – the variety of the passing scene. But the lack of visual diversion threw into relief the sounds and smell of the night-time canal. The splash of steering poles, the rustle of rats, and the pungent smell of compost heaps and smouldering autumn-leaf fires from the gardens of the big houses in Noel Road which hung above them to their right.

Too soon, came the long, narrow, Islington Tunnel. Pit dark with foul air and as silent as death. Once in there, the only sound to break the eerie stillness was the occasional splosh of sludge dropping into the water from the slimy ceiling. The glow from the narrow-boat cabin fires and oil lamps seemed to add to the oppressive atmosphere rather than relieve it – throwing sinister shadows on to the dank brick walls.

'In the sweet by-and-by, we shall meet by that beautiful shore,' sang out a lone voice from a boat up ahead. The refrain was picked up by William Taylor, Baxton's ebullient assistant, and then gradually the rest of the line joined in until their song reverberated all around them, warming them like a cloak. They often sang their way through the tunnel. American revivalist hymns were favourites, their throbbing melancholy seeming somehow most suitable.

'Gather with the saints at the river, that flows by the throne of God!' shouted Taylor encouragingly when silence overtook them again. Soon they were back in full and glorious song, but, as the end of the tunnel drew near, they remembered to tail off to a whisper. The cottagers who lived just by the exit did not feel the same need for the Lord's comfort in the early hours. They might complain again and company jobs were precious. As it happened, most land-bound folk regarded canal boatmen as Godless and immoral. But, if hymns are any help in gaining entrance to the Kingdom of Heaven, they may have eased the way of some later that night.

The Islington Tunnel behind them, the little fleet glided silently by the towering warehouses huddled around the Battlebridge basin and approached the lair of their arch rivals – the railways. Here, the lines of the Midland went both under and over the canal and the railway goods yards were all around them – enemy country. It was starting to rain again as St Pancras double lock and basin came into view.

A hive of activity day and night, this was where the railways and canals pretended they were not engaged in a deadly war and exchanged goods for destinations only served by the other.

Some of the smells wafting towards Baxton's boat were pleasanter now: newly sawn timber, rich and cloying brewery malt and the peculiar sweetness of curtains of macaroni hung out to dry, which intermingled with less attractive odours from the canal itself and the reek of benzoline from their own cargo.

Soon be time for breakfast. Baxton smiled in anticipation at the thought. Meanwhile, the lad was brewing up. At one time there had been talk of banning their small fires and lamps but common sense had prevailed. How could they operate without them? They needed the light to see what they were doing and to brew up – never mind give them a little warmth in the cabins on the damp and bitter nights. Their life was hard enough already.

Additional little fireflies of light emanated from boatmen's pipes, but 35-year-old Baxton had never been a smoker. Now that Mary and the kids were living on land, he needed all his money to help keep them there. Charlie and Lizzie were actually going to school and it was the image of Lizzie reading aloud to him from a Sunday school tract that helped keep him going on this endless trail. His children would be able to read. Anything would be possible then. No narrow-boatman could wish for more. That, and breakfast soon.

An easy and quiet section of canal led up to Kentish and Camden Towns' timber yards and foundries and the hardest part of the night's work; a triple set of double locks. These they entered two by two, giving the crews the chance to have a gossip on the quayside between tasks.

They were making good time was the general opinion. Loads were discussed and compared and the cussedness of the City Quay loaders deplored. It was clear who had the heaviest load – Baxton. Good thing his boat was in the middle. Edward Hall, the dashing skipper of the *Limehouse*, asked William Taylor, Baxton's cheerful second man, whether he had noticed the stunned look on the face of the foreman of the railyard when he saw how heavy-laden they were? Taylor said he had and both men laughed at the memory. Typical landsman. Typical railway man. Thought he knew better.

On their way again, the convoy was soon riding a long curve north-westwards. Baxton, Taylor and the lad took it in turns to man the tiller and eat breakfast. A rapid succession of bridges looming darkly overhead as they did so: the Southampton, the Gloucester Avenue, the Grafton and, finally, Water Meeting Bridge.

Water Meeting Bridge was the scene of their trickiest manoeuvre. The *Ready* led its string of narrowboats into a sharp right turn as they entered the wider canal which curved around the north side of Regent's Park.

'That's a mighty heavy load, there,' remarked a policeman to his fellow constable as the middle bead of the necklace emerged from beneath Water Meeting Bridge. The steamtug was already out of sight around the corner so, the PC was later to state in evidence, he was unable to confirm whether it was puffing out showers of sparks at the time. He did notice, however, that smoke was issuing from the cabin chimney of the *Tilbury*.

The tricky right turn negotiated, the steerers, or the captains as they liked to call themselves, drew a collective sigh of relief. Shoes off, time to take breath. No more locks for a while, no tricky turns, just the peaceful, almost rural, surroundings of Regent's Park. At sparse intervals, the footbridges of the Outer Circle passed overhead and only the occasional animal call from the Regent's Park Zoo broke the night silence. The captains began to look to their bunks.

Indeed, just before it happened, Edward Hall, captain of the *Limehouse* which rode just behind the *Tilbury*, had already undressed and was snuggling down on his straw pallet.

Patients at the nearby Hospital for Nervous Diseases were fast asleep, as were most of the rich and famous in the elegant St John's Wood villas which overlooked the park and canal – among their number the well-known poisons expert, Professor Alfred Swaine Taylor, and many of 'The Wood' artistic colony. Not at home, however, was the colony's flamboyant and enormously successful leader, Lawrence Alma-Tadema, who painted lightly clad maidens reclining in Roman bath-houses in a manner which encouraged wealthy Victorian males to take a sudden interest in all things ancient. He was away in Scotland, quite unaware of the calamity about to overtake his appropriately Pompeian-style villa.

Just before it happened, the night gatekeeper of the North Lodge adjacent to Macclesfield Bridge (quite the most handsome on the Regent's Canal) went off duty. The son of the lodge-keeper, however, was lying on his bed fully clothed having got up too early for his task of taking the park gardeners' morning roll call.

Just before it happened, there appeared to be some problem on board Baxton's boat. A flash of light, shouts, fire, smoke.

Then it happened.

With a blinding flash and a roar so loud it was heard in Bermondsey, Peckham Rye and even faraway Chislehurst, Baxton's boat exploded.

For a mile around, the shock waves caused beds to rock to and fro, doors and shutters to burst open, glass to shatter, ceilings to fall, plaster to fly and the panic-stricken occupants to rush into the streets, fearing an earthquake – or the end of the world. Fortunately, *The Times* was later to report, when it happened most people were lying down 'in the position which soldiers are taught to assume to avoid the force of explosives'.

As Baxton's boat exploded, it was passing under Macclesfield Bridge – not only the most handsome on the canal but also quite the most sturdily built. Slabs of stone-facing, decorative iron railings and ten fluted, cast-iron columns were hurled into the air. With them, went the cargo of Baxton's boat, kerbstones and fencing from the towpath, canalside trees and portions of the roof and wall of the North Lodge which then smashed down on the nearby buildings. In particular, they smashed down on Holford Park, a huge mansion on the south side, and, on the north, the villa of Mr Alma-Tadema with its Latin greeting *Salve* inscribed on the lintel.

Like Mr Alma-Tadema's servants and children, the other narrow-boat captains had been lying down in a blast-avoiding manner. That of Jane, which led the procession, suddenly felt his sons crashing down on him, while the master of the Dee found himself in the water. Edward White, the captain of the *Limehouse*, was knocked out of his bed against the stove and, as his craft sank beneath him, lost consciousness.

At the zoo, *The Times* later reported, the monkeys appeared to have successfully avoided the falling glass. But the giraffes were found huddled together in terrible fear while the elans, true to their timid nature, 'suffered very much from their panic'.

Much of what had been hurled into the air by the violent explosion had come straight down again to land in the canal and on what remained of Baxton's boat. Once there, the earth and debris acted as a dam, cutting the canal into two separate stretches of water. Perched crazily on top of the 20-foot-high pile of wreckage were the fluted iron columns, spilling out their brick fillings.

At dawn, boatmen and firemen were to be seen poking about with poles and grappling hooks in the now shallow water around the sunken *Limehouse* and the fragments of Baxton's boat.

Hundreds of sightseers peered down on the scene from the high canal banks and over the raw edges of what had once been a bridge. Some held umbrellas to keep off the slanting rain which, along with the steady spillage from a fractured water-main and drainage pipe, was turning the piled soil into a muddy, slippery morass. Flames shooting from a broken gas main added a mournful glow to the grey, early morning scene.

Policemen and guardsmen from the nearby barracks tried to keep the growing crowd in check and out of danger as they craned forward so as not to miss any part of this terrible scene.

The almost holiday atmosphere abated momentarily and the crowd grew silent as rescuers staggered uncertainly up the slope supporting two covered stretchers carrying the bodies of William Taylor and the lad. Of skipper Baxton there was no sign. It wasn't until four in the afternoon, just as the rain eased a little, that the searchers came upon a solid object trapped beneath the remains of the *Limehouse*: the mangled body of Charles Baxton. A gruesome bonus for those who had braved the rain to keep watching or had just arrived on one of the special Regent's Park Explosion omnibus outings.

Now that all the victims had been accounted for and there was only merchandise to be retrieved, the work proceeded with less urgency. The gathering dusk slowed it further and some helpers began to call it a day.

It was then that they found the fourth body.

Chapter Two

Sergeant Ernest Best of the Detective Branch contemplated the bodies lined up on marble slabs and exclaimed, 'What do you mean, you don't know who they are! They worked for you, didn't they?'

'Only the captain,' said the Grand Junction Canal traffic manager shaking his head. 'He takes on his own crew.' He shrugged his gaunt shoulders. 'All we ask is that there are at least three of them.'

Best sighed. That made things very difficult. How was he going to begin on identifying the extra body if no one knew who the bona fide corpses were? It seemed ridiculous. 'But surely the other bargees know who they are?'

'No, not really.' Thornley paused, then corrected Best carefully, 'The *boatmen* come from all over the place.' The Sergeant said nothing and waited. The man looked unhappy, as if suspecting that much of this trouble was going to come right down on his head. 'They meet up here and there at the locks.' He tugged at the stiff collar constraining his scrawny neck. 'But don't necessarily get to know each other's names.' He paused before adding, 'Well, not their real names anyway. Sometimes, just their nicknames.'

'Because they're on the run?'

Best knew that, like the railway construction sites, the canals had a reputation for giving sanctuary to men who had good reason for forgetting their real names.

'No, not necessarily.' The traffic manager looked mildly offended. 'There's not as much of that as people think, you know. A lot of them are good family men. It's just, well, it's just their way.'

They were in the mortuary of the Marylebone Workhouse which Charles Dickens had described as 'a kind of crypt devoted to the warehousing of parochial coffins'. The mournful Thornley looked right at home in such bleak surroundings but Sergeant Best did not. It was not so much the vividness of his black hair or his extraordinary greeny-grey eyes and immaculate clothes, but the strong feeling of life emanating from him – despite his serious concentration on police business. Despite even the deep sadness at the heart of him.

'The boatmen think he might be Birmingham Joe – or Jack,' offered Thornley, pointing to the youngest and most badly burned of the three stocky bodies. 'But, I don't know . . . the lads are the hardest to recognize. So many of them – and they come from . . . well, from all over,' he trailed off.

The three bodies lying before them on the marble slabs had been sluiced down to remove some of the grey canal mud. It was a warm day and as the water drained off and the dampness evaporated they started to look more human. Hair began to spring away from heads and cheeks in a disconcerting manner and clothing to take on its proper hue. Best preferred bodies not to look so human.

'Let's start with the man you *do* know, shall we?' he said briskly. 'This is the captain, yes?'

Suddenly, tears welled into Thornley's eyes. He was touched, Best suspected, by genuine pity at the sight of Baxton's badly burned hands and smashed skull – and the heavy knowledge of the trouble the Grand Junction Canal, and thus himself, could be in.

Signalling young PC Smith to follow him with his notebook, Best snapped out, 'Charles Baxton? Yes?'

Thornley pulled himself up and responded, 'Yes. Charles Baxton. Been working for us for – for quite a few years.

In his mid-thirties, I'd say, and he's from Loughborough, in Leicestershire.'

'Family?'

Thornton nodded sadly. 'Yes. Wife and four children, too, they tell me.'

'God rest his soul.'

'Yes.'

'And this one? What have you got?'

Alongside the remains of Charles Baxton was the body of a man in early middle-age. One side of his face was adorned with mutton-chop whiskers, the other was merely raw flesh.

Thornley glanced at his notebook. 'The men say they think his name might be Tailford or Taylor. The captain of the *Dee* thinks he might be from Braunston or Brierley Hill.'

'Where's that?'

'I'm not sure. Leicestershire, I think.'

'Make sure you get *all* the details of these clothes,' Best murmured to Smith. 'This is fustian,' he said, feeling the man's dark jacket. 'And don't forget the buttons – whether they are brass or bone and so on. It's specially important when their clothes are so similar.' It was a lesson Best had learned from bitter experience.

PC John George Smith looked up from his notebook and nodded earnestly. He realized he probably knew more about clothes than the Sergeant ever would but he was grateful just to be there. Having been specially selected merely on the basis of his good handwriting and tolerable spelling, he was anxious to make the most of this opportunity.

When they came to the lad, the traffic manager could offer no suggestions apart from, 'Maybe Birmingham Joe,' again.

A silence fell on them as they stood before the woman's body. Her hair was fair, her body young and slight but her face had been destroyed. Relatives attempting to identify her were in for a terrible shock, thought Best. As disfigured as she was there was still, somehow, an air of prettiness about her – or delicacy rather. Certainly her fair hair and white skin came as a marked contrast to the rest of the group who were all stocky, muscular and as dark as gypsies.

Best broke the silence by enquiring bluntly, 'Baxton's wife – or woman d'you think?'

'Oh, no. Neither.'

'How on earth can you be so sure?'

'Women aren't allowed on board.'

Best was incredulous. 'You're not telling me I haven't seen dozens of women on these boats?'

'Not these particular boats,' corrected Thornley, his voice gaining confidence from the fact that he was at last able to speak with some authority. 'You would have seen them on *family-run* boats, not on company boats like these. We only employ men, and no strangers are allowed on board – particularly women.'

His blind faith puzzled Best who had never heard of a rule which didn't get broken. 'Not beyond the realms of possibility that he would give his woman a ride, though, is it?'

Thornley reddened and shook his head. 'You've seen the size of the cabins on these fly boats. The whole craft has to be especially narrow to get through the canals going north and with a full crew and such a heavy load ... '

'Wouldn't be absolutely *impossible*, though, would it? I'll grant you she may be a bit young to be his wife but she could be his daughter, though, or more likely ... '

Thornley shook his head and said firmly, 'One thing I do know, she *couldn't* have been on board at City Road.'

'All right,' Best conceded. He felt sorry for the man. 'But you don't see what's going on once they're underway, do you?' he added softly.

There was a strained silence. Thornley clearly did not want to make an enemy.

He was rescued by PC Smith who murmured quietly, 'Seems quite good quality, this petticoat, sir?'

Best glanced at what once had been plain white petticoats prinked with pale blue ribbons, then switched his surprised gaze to the constable. 'You experienced in these matters, Smith?'

John George blushed. 'No, sir. Well, I mean, the lace and everything – seems quite expensive.' He pointed to one of the silky blue ribbons, now recovering some of their sheen having been released from their muddy coating. 'New, don't you think, sir?'

Best continued to gaze bemusedly at the well-set-up Smith. Maybe the lad was merely very observant and thus a potential new local detective. God knows they needed some with some brains. Or maybe this handsome, blond, blue-eyed young lad just enjoyed fingering ladies underwear. Folks were funny, he had discovered since he joined the Force. Much funnier than he had ever imagined and rarely what they appeared to be.

'My mother takes in washing, sir,' Smith offered helpfully, 'from quite well-to-do people. So, when I lived at home I saw a lot of clothes . . . '

The Sergeant contemplated this intelligence for a few moments before saying, 'Well, young man, I think your mother should come in and give us her considered opinion on this underwear before we issue the description to the newspapers, don't you?'

'Yes, sir,' PC Smith gulped.

'And . . . '

'Yes, sir?'

'No word about this to anyone.'

'Oh no, sir. Of course not.'

'As far as the newspapers are concerned we have no suspicion she might have been on one of the boats. She just happened to be in the canal when it was dragged.

After all,' he said, reasoning with himself, 'she could just be a suicide. Plenty of people throw themselves into the canals. Might have gone in somewhere else and been dragged along by a boat. She could have been on the bridge when it exploded,' he went on. 'Doesn't seem to be burned, does she?' he asked suddenly.

Smith shook his head.

'Be interesting to know if she is with child, though, wouldn't it?'

Smith didn't know whether he was supposed to respond to this so confined himself to a guarded nod, hoping that his mother was not supposed to divine this as well.

'While we're waiting for the good surgeons to reveal all, we'll get some plain-clothes men out and about talking to the boatmen and the artistic folk of St John's Wood – see if anyone is missing. But discreetly, mind you. You know what people are.'

PC Smith couldn't believe his luck, 'You mean I can come too, sir?'

Best grinned. 'I do.'

The now quietly plain-clothed PC Smith in a modest, dark-grey suit, and the not-so-discreetly garbed Sergeant Best surveyed the scene of the explosion and had to agree that the Press were right. What had saved the pretty little Italianate villas and whitewashed Gothic houses from utter devastation was that they had been set well back from the Regent's Canal deep cutting. Nonetheless, in such an oasis of peace and sylvan rural charm such an occurrence must have seemed doubly shocking.

Best knew that St John's Wood was a mecca for artists and writers. He had read how James Tissot dispensed iced champagne to his wealthy patrons at his leafy Grove End villa. He had also seen paintings in which lightly clad languid and comely Grecian and Roman young ladies were draped against Doric columns or on tiger-skin rugs – all rumoured to have been posed in Lawrence Alma-Tadema's spacious garden or in his remarkable oriental studio.

The idea of meeting such people was exciting and, PC Smith had to admit, the mildly Bohemian-looking Sergeant Best probably fitted into this background better than he did. But he still found it hard to get used to the way Best's smile would suddenly flash and his eyes sparkle when he was amused or his interest had been aroused. Best seemed aware of the uneasiness his foreign-seeming vivacity engendered, for no sooner had his face lit up than he would suddenly switch off the lamp, letting his mouth harden a little – which, had he known it, only served to buttress the impression of quixotic foreignness.

Smith had been somewhat reassured, however, by the man from Scotland Yard's instant and businesslike, 'Now, it's "Sergeant" not "sir". You come with me, I need your local knowledge,' leaving the lazy and slovenly Sergeant in charge of the local detectives and crony constables to make their own way. Then, flatteringly, 'Where shall we start – John George, isn't it?'

'Yes, sir – Sergeant. But George will do.' Unaccustomed to being asked for his opinion, Smith hesitated before saying firmly, 'At Mr Alma-Tadema's, I think, Sergeant. He's an important man among all these artists so I expect his servants know what goes on around here.'

Best looked at him and laughed. 'You will go far, young Smith. Servants are the fount of all knowledge. Our biggest problem is hiding this fact from their masters!'

The Alma-Tadema villa appeared unlikely to present the pair with that problem. It was in such a sorry state that it was doubtful that anyone was at home. More suited to southern Italy's sunny skies, even when intact, its broken outline now looked forlorn against the grey and drizzling background of a miserable October day in London – a fact which was affording the newspapers untold delight. Cutting pretentious foreigners down to size was a favourite national sport.

To add a droll note, the famous artist's garden was now littered with nuts. Nuts had been among the lighter items in the *Tilbury*'s load and, consequently, had scattered further and wider than heavier merchandise. The two officers now contemplating this odd scene were unaware that nestling among the almonds and peanuts were tiny pellets of blasting powder – which looked remarkably similar to nuts.

Two lines of stakes had been driven into the canal demarking the edges of the disaster area. The gap between these stakes was tightly packed with cinders, forming waterproof barriers. Then the pumping-out began. Workmen followed the retreating water down the banksides, clearing the debris, and slipping and sliding in the mud as they did so.

Back in the Marylebone Workhouse the inquest on the accident had opened. The jury retired at once to the mortuary to view the bodies and listen as Baxton and Taylor were identified by fellow boatmen and company clerks. No such help could yet be given as to the identity of the third crew member, the young lad – or of the young woman. All the boatmen expressed total disbelief that Baxton would, or could, have smuggled her on board.

The coroner asked Edward Hall, steerer of the *Limehouse*, what he thought might have caused the explosion.

'Lightning,' he answered promptly. 'There was a lot of it about that night.' He nodded. 'A lot.'

Answers to questions about the exact contents of Baxton's boat were less prompt and precise. In fact they proved quite vague.

'Oh, you know – a few nuts and other things,' offered a labourer who had witnessed the loading, 'Some sugar, some bags, and some casks of – of all sorts.'

'But what did the casks *contain*?' enquired the coroner testily.

'I don't exactly know.' The man looked about him desperately searching for help. 'No, I don't know,' he repeated firmly when he saw he was on his own then mumbled something half to himself.

'What did you say, man? Speak up! Speak up!'

'I said, Your Lordship,' he muttered miserably, 'that it's more than my place is worth to know.'

As Best and Smith expected, Mr Alma-Tadema was not at home. But a neighbour was. He was a Mr Van Ellen, a stout, middle-aged banker with a very smooth, pink-and-white skin and cherubic features. In contrast, his manner was precise to the point of abruptness, probably, surmised Best, to stop you taking his babylike features at face value. He in turn had made it clear that he was relieved that, despite Best's mildly *outré* appearance, he was not 'one of those daubers'.

'No, Sergeant, neither I nor my family have heard about any young lady being missing.'

The Sergeant doubted whether the family had been asked. 'Perhaps, sir,' he said mildly, 'the ladies, not being as busy as yourself, may have heard of some servant problem or ...?'

'Oh, that's most unlikely, Officer,' said the banker dismissively. 'Most unlikely. You see, they have very little to do with our neighbours.' He made the word sound pejorative.

Best firmed up his voice so that a refusal would tend to lead to confrontation, something he suspected from which the foreign-born Mr Van Ellen would shrink. 'I assure you that sometimes the most seemingly unimportant information can be of assistance.' There was an awkward silence. 'And I'm sure the commissioner would be most obliged for your assistance,' he added. Thus implying that Van Ellen was on intimate terms with Colonel Sir Edmund Henderson while hinting that co-operation with the police was the decent English thing to do.

'Very well, Officer,' he shrugged, 'I am persuaded.' He picked up a silver handbell from a side table, then added suddenly, 'But I'm sure you would be better employed talking to some of my neighbours who seem to have ladies coming and going with great regularity.' He paused, suddenly aware that his remark might seem improper, 'As artists' models, of course.'

'Of course, sir, of course. We will be talking to everyone.' Over Van Ellen's shoulder, he could see into Alma-Tadema's garden. Glinting in the weak sun on the far side was the windowed wall of what he guessed was the artist's studio. Was the banker jealous of these artists who were flouting convention, getting away with it – and becoming very wealthy in the process? Or was the ire more personal? Had, perhaps, the colourful Alma-Tadema been attracting the notice of the ladies of the Van Ellen household?

After Van Ellen had given the crisply pinnied parlour-maid her instructions to rally the family, Best murmured casually, 'And, perhaps, while I am talking to the ladies, Constable Smith could be having a brief word with the servants?'

'Oh, I really don't think they could possibly know anything,' said Van Ellen in a manner which doubtless brooked no refusal at his bank.

Best nodded as though agreeing, but added, man-to-man, 'Unfortunately, I do have to assure the commissioner that I have been absolutely thorough. You understand my problem, sir. And servants do tend to know other servants – so it's always possible ... ' he shrugged, 'just a formality.' He pushed Smith after the retreating parlour-maid as though the arrangement was a foregone conclusion. 'Your family consists of, sir?'

As though in answer, two ladies entered the room. One was a tall, apologetically plain, young girl; the other a homely, though quite handsome, middle-aged woman encased in a dark-red dress heavily embroidered in black and set off with masses of jet jewellery – all of which rather overwhelmed her.

While they were being introduced as Van Ellen's wife and daughter, a young man wearing city clothes and a pained expression came into the parlour – carelessly letting the door bang behind him. His expression did not improve on meeting Best. 'I would have thought you could be better employed keeping that rabble outside in order. It really is too much. The omnibus companies are running special excursions, for God's sake!'

'Roger usually enjoys walking along the canal towpath in the evenings,' said Mrs Van Ellen by way of excusing his rudeness. 'It helps him to relax after his day in the city.'

This did not please Roger either. He coloured up and snapped, 'Mother, you do exaggerate. I only go down there occasionally.'

Now why would that bother you, wondered Best? It came as no surprise to him that the young man, familiar as he was with the canal, could offer no suggestions as to whose body the fourth victim might be. 'Apart from some silly maidservant finding herself in trouble!' Best wanted to punch him. No, he had not been on the towpath the previous evening. He had been dining out in St James's.

Best was not sorry when the parlour-maid reappeared with a message that a constable had called and left word that he should return to the Yard – at once.

Chapter Three

'It's murder,' announced Chief Inspector Cheadle, 'and you've got the docket.'

He tapped the narrow, folded document which lay on top of others on the crowded desk now lit by some welcome, early evening sun. 'She was stabbed,' he added bluntly.

Best braced himself for the gory details but Cheadle continued, 'You've started on the job already so you might as well stay on it. Anyway,' he said drily, 'we'll need somebody a bit fancy to handle them artistic fellows.'

'Yes, sir.' Cheadle was nothing if not gracious, thought Best.

'It might tie up with that Thames case an' you know a bit about that.'

They were sitting in the Inspectors' room of the Detective Branch at Great Scotland Yard, home to three Chief Inspectors and three Inspectors – all out on various cases.

'There's going to be a lot of legwork so we'll need some more 'elp.' Cheadle sighed. 'You know how these bodies in the water are – could come from anywhere. Give me a good thief, you know what to expect.'

Cheadle regarded himself as a good, honest thief-taker, and the likes of Best as lacking not only the necessary experience but the natural 'nose' for the job. Not for the first time Best was grateful that at least he had not come straight into the department. True, he had not worn uniform for very long before his knowledge of languages had channelled him towards the Yard, but enough to avoid the 'direct entry – know nothing' slur. In fact, he had rather enjoyed the street life and camaraderie of common constables, but he doubted whether Cheadle would have believed that.

'Can we have PC Smith and some of the Special Patrols?'

Cheadle grimaced, pulling at his sandy side whiskers. 'Divisionals won't like it, you know.'

'Young Smith was in at the start, sir, and he's very keen.'

He didn't add that Smith could compose reasonable reports, while some divisional detectives could scarcely write their names. It would scarcely have been tactful, given the Chief Inspector's own drawbacks in that area. Tales of Cheadle's latest grammatical errors and spelling howlers were a source of great entertainment to the Sergeants' office.

'I'll speak to his superintendent.' He paused then said, 'Right, what's your tale so far, Sergeant Best?'

As plainly as he could and avoiding any fancy words Best described his actions so far.

'Obviously we've been concentrating on positive identification of the boy and the woman,' he said, giving the word 'positive' careful emphasis.

Cheadle suddenly shot upright in his chair in a manner which had frightened many a poor rookie detective half to death. The receiver's issue chairs were not suitable support for such a big and burly man with the result he gradually slipped down in them.

'Have a word with Sayer – get the latest on the Thames case. He's out having a look at another bit – part of the head, I think.'

Best hesitated.

'What?'

'Why would he cut up the first body but not the second?'

'Depends how much time he had, laddie, doesn't it? Might have intended to, but' – Cheadle spread his huge hands – 'he ran out of time. Right', continued the still very upright Chief Inspector, 'let's put the pictures in their frames, shall we? Picture number one: the murder happened near the canal and she was shoved straight in. Picture two:'

– he counted off on his thick, reddened fingers – 'she was murdered on the *Tilbury* or that other barge what sunk.'

'The *Limehouse*, sir.'

'The *Limehouse*,' echoed Cheadle. Best refrained from mentioning that they were known as canal boats, not barges.

'Picture three: she was done in before being put on one of the barges; and picture four: she was dumped in somewhere else on the canal and she got caught up on one of the barges and dragged along.' He paused. 'You think of any other pictures, Sergeant?'

'No, sir. Oh, apart from the possibility that she might have been on the bridge when the explosion occurred.'

'At 5 a.m.?' He frowned. 'Do prostitutes do business there?'

'Not sure, sir. I'm checking.'

'Right. Let's go back to picture one. The murder happened near the canal and she was shoved straight in.'

'Seems to be a big coincidence that she was murdered on the same night as the explosion.'

'Could have happened some time before.'

'Not long before – the body is quite fresh.'

'That don't necessarily mean that much,' Cheadle declared. 'Might have been tucked away somewhere cool. Keep a look out for somewhere cool.' Best wondered how he was going to do that. 'Ask the bargees, they'll know about the water temperature in the different parts.'

Best nodded.

'Any missing women thereabouts?'

'Not heard of anyone so far, sir. But so many women come and go from those houses: artists' models, ladies sitting for their portraits – and there are quite a few actresses and singers in the area.'

'A few very fancy ladies, too, I hear,' interposed Cheadle. Some of the best-kept, kept women resided in St John's Wood.

'Yes sir. But it's usually the men who come and go from them.'

They shared a conspiratorial, male laugh.

'An' if one of them ladies got difficult. . . ?'

'Possibility sir. But I think that the victim seems more likely to have been a boatman's woman – or a servant.'

'Why's that?'

'Well,' he began carefully, 'Smith's mother says the petticoats are made of very good material, sir, and trimmed with expensive lace – but not new.'

'Smith's mother! She on the payroll as well, then?'

Best grinned apologetically. 'No, sir, she takes in washing, sir, and knows about these things.'

Cheadle looked amused. He was a firm believer in the superiority of the working classes.

'Which either means,' Best continued, 'the woman was wealthy, or–'

'Or she had them passed on. You don't have to paint me a picture, Sergeant. So she could be a lady's maid . . . '

'Or even a real lady fallen on hard times. And then there are her hands, sir. Mrs Smith,' he went on, doggedly avoiding Cheadle's eye, 'says they are not a lady's hands or those of someone used to heavy manual work.'

Back to that old question. In the Thames case, the newspapers had made much of the fact that the hands had not yet been found. These, they declared 'would at least have revealed the victim's station in life'. It was almost as if it were the fault of the police that the the river had not yet given them up.

'So, something in between, eh? Not quite a lady, not quite a skivvy?'

'Yes. Someone who at least has to look after herself.'

'So, could be a governess, a lady's maid, an artist's model, or even a shopkeeper?' said Cheadle, 'Anyway, let's look at picture number four – her being dragged along by one of the barges.' He scratched his head. 'Though I got to admit that it does seem a bit unlikely that she could have been carried far without being spotted at one of the locks and there's nothing in the post-mortem report about any crush injuries the body could have got from a barge.'

'Might have been protected by the dress, sir, which then got pulled off?'

'Maybe. But I don't think so. I think whoever killed her pulled her dress off and she went in where she was found. The simplest explanation is usually the right one. Just for now, though, let's put our money on pictures one to three.' He paused, 'Speaking of pictures, got any photographs yet?'

'I'm getting them done of the boy, but I think the woman's face is too badly damaged to be recognized, sir.'

'Pity. Maybe the reward notices will turn up something – they nearly ready?'

'Just sent them for printing, sir.'

'Good.' Cheadle nodded and took out his watch. Best got up to go but the Chief Inspector held up his hand, 'You realize there is a fifth possibility.'

'Sir?'

'She might have had something to do with the explosion.' Best was puzzled. 'We don't know what caused it yet, do we?'

'No sir, but—'

'Could have been deliberate, couldn't it?'

'Yes, I suppose so.' He frowned. 'Do you mean the Fenians sir?' God forbid they were back in business.

'Hm. Mebbe. Mebbe.' He shrugged. 'Or, mebbe some rival. Have you thought of that?' Best hadn't. 'Or,' he paused and stared meaningfully over his metal-rimmed spectacles, 'the Grand Junction company themselves.'

'Sir?'

'In business difficulties – you knows the picture . . . ' He tapped his nose. 'Sniff around.'

Cheadle might be the most ill-educated man at the Yard, but he was also the most astute. That thought was to reoccur as Best 'sniffed around' among the piles of debris which had been brought up the bank from the canal. And the smell was not sweet. It was all such a mess, but he could discern scraps of tarpaulin, torn sacks (some, miraculously, still half full of nuts or sugar), oildrums and, pathetically, a battered tin mug.

'Seen this?' enquired the tweed-suited Home Office explosives expert. He scraped at the mud on one of the oil drums better to reveal its markings: 'Hayes & Co., Boston, USA.' They looked at each other.

'Fenians?'

He shrugged. 'Could be.'

At one time *any* explosion had been followed by the immediate Press cry, 'Another Fenian Outrage!' Hardly surprising. In the space of two years, a number of bombings and shootings had been carried out by this Irish—American freedom movement. The last outrage, the Clerkenwell Prison Explosion, had been almost seven years ago. Since then, silence. Recent reports from across the Atlantic had informed them not only was the movement still flourishing but also plotting more mayhem. They hadn't expected it this soon.

Best sighed and added Fenians to his growing list of suspects.

HER SOUL WILL ROT IN HELL! The words raged across the wall of the St Pancras lock-keeper's cottage in huge malignant letters, splashes of whitewash dripping down the brickwork and spreading over the canalside paving. It was not the only message. Further along, in smaller and slightly calmer lettering, was the claim, SHE HAS GONE TO SATEN!, and the imperative instruction, SINNERS REPENT!

'When did they appear?' enquired Best.

'No one knows,' replied Thornley. 'They were noticed at first light.'

'So, any time during the night.'

Thornley nodded tiredly. 'Not when the fly boats were passing through, though – someone would have seen.'

'The question is, are they talking about our victim and, if so, who is the message meant for? Can't be for the other boatmen.'

Smith looked puzzled.

'They can't read,' Best explained.

'Oh, one or two of them can,' exclaimed Thornley, then admitted, 'Well, a little bit anyway.'

They turned back to the venomous messages. It was extraordinary how hate and evil could permeate the atmosphere from mere words. It was depressing. Particularly because the feelings expressed seemed so strangely at odds with the pathetic, unclaimed little body Best had so recently seen lying on a cold slab in Marylebone Workhouse. 'The phrasing is a bit Biblical – like . . . '

'One of them religious tracts?' offered Thornley.

'Yes.'

'Those Bible thumpers are always trying to save the boatmen.' He shook his head in wonderment.

'So, the writer *might* be a boatman, just be copying something he's seen?'

'But then why didn't they get Satan right?' asked Smith. Then answered his own question. 'Maybe doing it from memory?'

Best nodded. 'Or,' he said, devilishly, 'they *could* really be educated but unable to spell, or educated but pretending not to be able to spell – just so as to fool us.'

Smith looked dazed.

'Not going to be an easy one this,' said Best. 'I feel it in my bones. Her soul will rot in hell! Sounds like a religious maniac murderer shouting in triumph, or maybe a frightened irreligious murderer trying to divert attention from himself – or, then again,' – he looked rueful – 'someone just amusing themselves at our expense. Anyway, I'll put evangelists on my list, just in case.'

'I've something else for your list,' broke in a doleful Thornley. 'It's just a rumour so far, mind you. You know how it is, things are said at the lockside and the boats pass on . . . ' Best waited patiently. 'Then they meet up with others and the story is exaggerated. Anyway, it's said that a fight between a man and a woman was heard here on the lockside on the night in question – just as the fly boats were passing through.'

Best got out his notebook.

The list of missing women had been whittled down to five possibles. Now, after further perusal, Best put three of these aside: one whose hair was described as 'mid-brown' and who, if her estimated height was right, was too short. Another, who had a prominent, curved scar on her left shoulder – their corpse had no such marking. The third was too old. That left two. One of these was a young seamstress from Streatham. But it was the second of the two who excited him. Her description was the nearest. 'And look where she lives!' he exclaimed, holding up the scribbled draft for the printed information leaflet:

£50 Reward
Missing

LIZA MOODY, aged 24, left the Three Tuns Public House, Stibbington Street, Somers Town, where she is a barmaid, at about 9 p.m. on Saturday, 30 September, 1874. Has not been seen since.

DESCRIPTION: height, 5 feet 2-3 inches, well proportioned, pale complexion, light hair and eyes. Dress:

dark-green stuff with black buttons and trim, red and green plaid shawl, green bonnet with hanging flowers.

Best slapped the notice excitedly, 'Somers Town – just by King's Cross!'

Smith coughed, and murmured apologetically, 'It does say the 30th there, doesn't it – or might it be the 20th? It's difficult to tell.'

Best had had the same thought but had pushed it away. If it was the 20th it was probably too early. They both peered hard at the spot where Sergeant Rogers' free hand became even freer.

'Better check the register,' Best snapped. 'No, I'll do it,' he stayed Smith with a peremptory gesture, 'I know where it is.' Ridiculously, he was cross at having his enthusiasm dampened even though he knew Smith was being sensible. He came back more long-faced.

'It was the 20th. Two weeks before our body was found.'

They sat in silence, contemplating this latest setback.

'She could have been held captive, or been on board all that time – voluntarily,' suggested Smith, wishing he hadn't burst the Sergeant's balloon. The man had looked so pleased. He was even beginning to appreciate that flashing smile. Brightened the day.

Best shook his head. 'Not on board for that long. Those cabins are so *small* – she would have been seen.'

'Well, she might have been seen by the boatmen, but would they have told us? My mother says they're as secretive as gypsies.'

The mercurial Best brightened. 'You could be right, young Smith. You could be right. If you *are* I'll buy you a pint of the best ale – and two for your mother. In the meantime, you go and find out more about Liza Moody of Somers Town. I will go and spirit some information out of the lock-keepers by threatening to reveal that they break canal company law by allowing prostitutes on the lock sides.'

'Do they?'

Best gave him an old-fashioned look. 'I don't know. But what would be your guess, young Smith?'

Chapter Four

'It could have devastated Islington, St Pancras or part of the Harrow Road district with twenty-five thousand inhabitants!' exclaimed the coroner. 'Houses there would go down like a pack of cards each taking with them three or four families!'

Dragging himself back from a predicted drama to the lesser one which had actually taken place, he reopened the inquest on the Regent's Canal Explosion.

Workhouses are already such depressing places, reflected Best, that holding inquests in them seems to be adding insult to injury. But at least the St Marylebone Workhouse was clean and had a reputation for being well run. The hearing took place in a sort of boardroom filled with horsehair-stuffed chairs so large and square that a previous inquest juror, Charles Dickens, had wondered for which race of Patagonians they had been made. At the moment the room was rather more overwhelmed by a surprising number of distinguished gentlemen – surprising given the humble origins of those whose deaths were being investigated.

There were Home Office and War Office explosives experts, solicitors and barristers representing the Regent's Canal Company, the Grand Junction Canal Company and persons whose property had been damaged by the explosion five days earlier. Indeed, the only persons who seemed to have no one speaking up or watching out for them were the victims and their relatives.

When they had all settled down, the coroner announced that given the seriousness of the matter their enquiry must extend to the carriage and storage of gunpowder.

It was now five days since the explosion and, disappointingly, they were still no further forward in identifying the young lad and woman. A failure Best felt keenly. He still thought that enquiries on the locksides regarding prostitutes might be profitable but his efforts had been cut short for the time being by the sudden necessity to attend the inquest where all he could do was listen to evidence of the causes of the explosion and hope this might throw up a clue.

Edward Hall, steerer of the *Limehouse*, was still sticking to lightning as his guess at the cause, but there was progress in another matter – the truth about the contents of the *Tilbury*'s cargo.

Gone was the pretence that it had merely carried nuts, sugar and other dry goods. With gunpowder scattered around the scene for all to see it could scarcely be denied that it had been part of the cargo. But the admission of just how much had been aboard the ill-fated vessel that night brought a gasp from onlookers and even raised eyebrows among the lawyers well accustomed to startling revelations. The *Tilbury* had been weighed down by no less than five tons of gunpowder.

The beady eyes of the explosives experts now focused on exactly how this dangerous substance was packaged and transported. Clearly they believed that even if it had been ignited by an act of God, such as a bolt of lightning, this was by no means the only cause. Their probing questions eventually brought admissions that while the 'sporting powder' was well packaged, the barrels containing blasting powder destined for Nottingham's coal mines were not strong. Indeed, the bottoms sometimes dropped out of them and when they did the gunpowder was just scooped up, put back in like so much sugar, and the barrel-bottoms tapped back into place.

Neither were there any special precautions taken in the carriage. It was loaded on to ordinary boats with ordinary iron fittings, by boatmen wearing their ordinary clothes and ordinary boots. The men were not searched for matches for there was no rule against smoking or having fires in the cabin. Even Best, uninitiated as he was in the finer points of goods transportation, could see the case for negligence relentlessly building up. And if they were that negligent about carriage, might not they also be similarly slack about other rules such as allowing no strangers on board?

'Were there any specific instructions about the carriage of gunpowder?' the Home Office man enquired coldly.

'No . . . just caution,' the steerer replied nervously and rather superfluously in the circumstances. Then he had second thoughts and added that they always put a cloth or tarpaulin over the gunpowder 'An' we don't do that with no other cargo. Oh, an' the boat is always watered before we put it in, but there was no need that night what with all the rain an' all.'

Just as Hall was conceding that cabin fires were forbidden, but only when they were carrying government explosives from arsenal to arsenal, Best slipped out into the corridor. There, the waiting witnesses offered a stark contrast to the bevy of top-hatted and frock-coated representatives and watchers inside.

Among them was the now bowler-hatted traffic manager, Albert Thornley, who sat nervously clutching a wooden model of a fly boat and the bills of lading which the coroner had instructed him to produce. His bony head was bent in anxious conference with the two workmen on either side of him.

Best walked straight past them and out to the front steps where he lit a cigarette and stood watching idly the stream of passers-by hurrying towards Madame Tussaud's Waxwork Exhibition intent on glimpsing the latest 'amazingly realistic' images of the Tsar of all the Russias, the late Mr Charles Dickens, and the judges in the sensational, long-running case of the Tichborne Claimant. He then turned his attention to the list of witnesses pinned up in the entrance.

By the time he had finished his cigarette and returned to the corridor, Thornley had gone into the inquest chamber to give his evidence. This allowed the Police Sergeant with the conveniently foreign air, to slip quietly into his now vacant seat.

At first, Best sat gazing blankly into the distance but, after a while, he began shifting about restlessly, and emitting just perceptible sighs. Then he began to tap the toe of one of his sleek, four-button boots on the shiny parquet floor.

'This is a liberty,' he murmured shaking his head, 'a liberty.' He stared about him, sighed, and pointed out a little more loudly, just what a waste of time it all was. 'We should all be in there, you know. Never mind all those toffs. Never mind no room. Inquests are public. We should be in there.'

The thin, rigid-faced man on his right ignored the detective's overtures and continued to stare morosely into the distance. But the stocky workman on Best's left nodded eager agreement. 'That's right. That's right!'

This would be loader Sam Grealey. Nervous, bored out of his mind, unable to engage his morose companion in conversation, and probably unable to enjoy the distraction of reading, for the simple reason that had never learned how. Grealey's nods of agreement seemed to set off a nervous reaction and his head was now juddering from side to side several times as he said, 'Goes on and on, don't it?'

'It's not as if I know anything of any use,' complained Best.

'Me, neither. Me, neither,' agreed Grealey. 'But it don't seem to make no difference, do it?'

'They think we've got nothing better to do,' said Best crossly as he extracted the *Graphic* from his jacket pocket, unfolded it at the sporting page and began to study the racing form. He would rather have read the nearby report on the bicycle races at Cremorne Gardens but reckoned that the horses would be more in Grealey's line.

'What's Hall been going on about in there?' Grealey asked abruptly, anxious to keep Best talking.

'Oh, I don't know – something about how they always water the boats before they put in the gunpowder – then cover it with tarpaulin . . . '

Grealey grinned knowingly. 'Is that right?'

'Not true?' murmured Best mildly as he refolded his paper into a smaller square to check the Newmarket form.

Grealey gave a sudden barking laugh which caused the other man to turn his head at last. 'Well, from what I've seen . . . ' An icy glance from the silent man stopped him in his tracks. 'It's, well, yes, that's how it is. Watering and everything,' he paused, confused. 'Don't have to do it when it rains though. No need, you see. Rain does it for you.'

'Well, dangerous stuff, isn't it, this gunpowder?' murmured Best non-committally and settled down with his pencil and the list of runners.

The other man turned his face away again. Grealey, discomfited but unwilling to lose contact, straightened up his bulky shoulders defiantly. 'Goin' to 'ave a bet then?'

'Just perusing the field,' said Best, 'just perusing. But I reckon I'd do it better with a smoke. Helps me think.' He got up and wandered back towards the entrance. He was holding a match to his second cigarette when Grealey appeared beside him. 'Got too much for you in there as well?' Best murmured, proffering his tin.

'No thanks, prefer something stronger,' said Grealey, fishing a brown holland bag and a packet of cigarette papers from his trouser pocket. 'By the bye, take no notice of me mate.' Grealey gestured back into the building with his upturned thumb, 'Joe Minchin. He's all right, really, but he's got a few things on his mind.'

'Isn't he the load-checker?'

'Right, right.'

'No wonder he's worried!'

'Oh yeah, yeah,' Grealey nodded then added in the manner of a man who enjoys knowing something others don't. 'But, 'course, it ain't just that.'

'No?' Clearly, Grealey wanted it teased out of him but Best played a waiting game.

'Some woman problem, they say,' he offered finally.

'Ain't it always,' shrugged Best. 'Ain't it always.' Glancing down as he put away his silver match case, the familiar engraving of intertwined Es caught the light and to his astonishment he felt a sudden and violent rush of tears.

Unaware, Grealey grinned. 'If they knew the trouble they caused us!'

Best nodded, unable to trust himself to utter.

'Here, you all right, mate?' asked the startled Grealey.

'Oh yes, yes. Must have caught a chill. Always makes my eyes water.' He blew his nose heartily wiping his eyes at the same time. After all this time it could still hit him like this – like an unprovoked punch in the face. Making life seem totally empty and pointless again, even when the thought of his lovely Emmy had not been in his conscious thoughts.

Grealey patted him on the shoulder, 'Nothing but trouble, mate, nothing but trouble.' The sentiment clearly affected him greatly as his head went into a paroxysm of twitches.

It was ironic, Best thought later, that after all his careful strategy it was his impromptu tears which had made safe his cover as far as Grealey was concerned.

When Best went back into the inquest chamber, the plain-spoken Brummie steerer of the steamboat which had tugged the fated fleet that night, was recalling hearing

someone shouting at him to stop. He went on to explain
that he didn't because he was used to men calling this out
in jest. A further call, 'Stop, this boat's afire!' had caused
him to ring his bell, stop his engine and turn around, in
time to catch, 'A beautiful blue bursticle of flame', lighting
up the bows of the *Tilbury*.

'Then it all went dark again. But I shouldn't think it
was hardly a minute later when it all went up – knocking
me against the cabin side. There was a blue flame – all the
pieces went across the bridge. Then a piece of the bridge
shifted a bit, and it all dropped.'

PC Smith wasn't making much progress with the affable
landlord of the Three Tuns in Somers Town. He obviously
felt he had already said everything there was to say about his
missing barmaid, Liza Moody, and was too busy or too lazy
to exercise his mind again on behalf of a fresh-faced young
constable. Smith could understand that. In any case, his brief
was to get the feel of the place, as well as to try to prise out
any more useful information. So, while the landlord went
off to serve customers, Smith sat quite cheerfully imbibing
a half a pint of ale and surveying his fellow customers.

They were an odd assortment, but then, it was an odd area
dominated by three huge and imposing railway termini:
King's Cross, Euston Station and the fantastic, castellated St
Pancras. The sordid and sooty corridor in between provided
down-at-heel hotels and lodging-houses. These catered
for the poorest of travellers and tenants such as French
and Spanish refugees who scraped a dire living in freezing
rooms by teaching and translating their native languages.

Right in the middle of the central corridor sat the
Three Tuns Public House which, despite its dowdy
surroundings, was cheerful with brass lamps and red plush.
Adding to the mixture of local residents and travellers were
oil-streaked railway workers and ebullient costermongers

from the rowdy street market nearby. And, of course, there were the prostitutes. It was one of the latter, a tiny, dark, cherry-cheeked, bright-eyed, 16-year-old whore, who sat herself down beside the handsome young policeman and began to talk to him.

First came the everyday comment that he was a stranger in these parts. This was quickly followed by the offer of her wares in a manner so outright and matter-of-fact that Smith laughed. She laughed too, thinking she had made a quick sale, but was soon sobered by his announcement that he was a police officer trying to help find Liza Moody. It had occurred to him that he might be on a fool's errand. He knew that bar staff tended to move from pub to pub and also that given the opportunities of the area Liza may have supplemented her meagre pay with some part-time prostitution and simply left to become a full professional. He voiced this thought to his young companion whose name, he had learned, was Maisie. She shook her head vigorously, 'No, no, m'dear,' she assured him in the manner of someone twice her age, 'not that Liza.'

Glancing around meaningfully he said, 'Well, I would have thought . . . '

'Well, you would have thought wrong, m'dear,' she interrupted him. 'I – knew that Liza. A darling girl but very innocent – straight from the farm. Knew everything there was to know about cows and pigs and all that stuff, but nothin' about men. They're the same thing, if you ask me.'

'Yes, but she might have been different with men. Some man could have got around her if she was innocent, like you say.'

She held up her hand to stop him, shaking her head vigorously, 'No, no. I'm telling you.' She paused, looked around and lowered her voice, 'In fact, there is something I *could* tell you.'

Smith leaned his ear down towards her expectantly.

'Here, you stop bothering the young constable.' The landlord stood before them wiping his hands. He did not have to tell Maisie twice. When Smith turned back she was gone.

'Sorry, I've been so long,' the landlord apologized, 'but I've got a minute now.' He leaned on the scrubbed counter, a fat Welshman with flat black hair which clung like a cap to his head giving him an oddly boyish look for a man who must be at least forty years old. 'Look, you know, I think you might as well stop looking for Liza.'

Smith was startled. 'You know where she is?'

'No, but, I mean I feel a bit of a fool saying she was missing at all. You know what barmaids are like. Here today, gone off tomorrow without so much as a ta ta – usually only stopping to grab some of the takings.' The man's features stayed quite immobile as he spoke giving no hint of what he was really thinking. 'You can see what it's like round here.' His hand lazily encompassed his dubious clientele. 'It's easy for the girls to start doing a bit of business on the side. Then some bloke gets them set up to do it full time . . . plenty of work from the railway stations, there is. I reckon that's what she's done.'

'You didn't think so at first.'

He shrugged. 'No, bit of a shock I suppose – probably because she didn't take nothing when she went. But now I've found a bit of cash has gone after all and then there was this man I saw her talking to . . . Well, that's what I reckon – don't you, boy?'

There was no sign of Maisie when Smith left. Found herself a customer, he smiled sadly to himself. There was one more task to complete before he headed back to the Yard. He checked his watch before walking to what he reckoned was the nearest point on the Regent's Canal which ran in a curve around the streets just north of Somers Town. It took him exactly ten minutes.

Chapter Five

The autumn was Best's favourite season but this one had so far failed miserably to live up to his expectations of crisp air and misty aspects. It was inappropriately warm for a start. It was also wet, very wet, and quite often foggy. The *Graphic* (his favourite newspaper for its numerous and dramatic illustrations) had been right in dubbing the month 'this soaking October'. Dreary, miserable, soaking October, they might have said.

His mercurial heart lightened a little as he entered the City Road Wharf of the Grand Junction Canal Company. Not only was it bustling with activity but it was well lit by gas and, unexpectedly, had a roof. At least he would be protected from the drizzle which had begun again just as he alighted from his cab.

The cabbie, who had conveyed Best from the Scotland Yard rank on many an odd quest, had been surprised by this destination and a little uncertain of its whereabouts. 'Don't get much call for that place you see, guv. Sure it will be open this time of day?'

That all this lively scene carried on daily without his awareness was also a matter of wonder to Best. Another world that he had been missing. He weaved his way between bales of wool and piles of boxes, barrels and casks stacked by the dark pool at the centre of the yard. All around, men moving, humping and straining as they shifted the goods. They had little breath left for pleasantries, but there were shouts of guidance to the hoist operators and the odd epithet – many of which Best could not decipher. The men used various Midland dialects interspersed with boatmen's language. Sounds foreign to me, he smiled to himself.

Trusting that the lack of comprehension worked only one way he enquired of one of the weathered boatmen as to the whereabouts of Mr Thornley. The man listened carefully, nodding his head, but his eyes were riveted on Best's gleaming boots. His own were no less extraordinary to Best's eyes. Like armoured men-of-war. Their incredibly thick leather was protected at both heel and toe with slabs of metal while, on the soles, hobnails so large that they gave the man an extra half an inch in height. How on earth did he manage to stay upright on them? Come to that, how could he feel the deck beneath him? One thing Best was sure of, if the boatman ever went overboard his amazing footwear must anchor him securely to the bottom. Perhaps there was a way of slipping out of them quickly? Best smiled to himself. Emma would have loved hearing about the boatman's boots.

The tall, gaunt Thornley, appeared more resigned to the calamity which had overtaken both him and his company but remained guarded in his responses. Best made clear that he was interested only in information relating to his murder enquiry, not the causes of the explosion. He also managed to infer that he believed this murder was nothing to do with the Grand Junction Canal Company, but that he needed their help to find out as much as possible about canals, boatmen and so on – just so he knew what he was talking about – and to please his boss.

It was a quarter truth, Best admitted to himself. While counting himself as an honest man, he knew that telling a few white lies was often the only way a policeman could get his job done. To lull Thornley further, the Sergeant produced his list of questions and launched into them with the innocuous, 'How often is the canal drained?'

'Once a year.'

'And the last occasion was . . . ?'

'Six months ago.'

'Can you tell me something about the boat people?'

'How d'you mean?' Thornley looked defensive. As he played for time, scratching the spot on the top of his head where the shiny scalp shone through the wispy hair, Best noticed for the first time that where Thornley's right thumb should have been was only a mutilated stump and across the palm a deep scar.

'I mean, generally,' Best murmured casually. 'Not just the ones you employ. You know, what kind of people are they? How do they live? That sort of thing. If you can just give me an idea, I'm a bit out of my depth here.'

Relieved, Thornley exclaimed, 'Well, they're not as bad as they're painted, I can tell you. They have a hard life, you know! That George Smith doesn't know what he's talking about!'

The philanthropist, George Smith, had recently turned his attentions from the plight of the brickyard children to the tribulations of the offspring of boatmen. Already perceived as having foul-mouthed and loose-living parents, he was claiming the children received no education and were ill-treated and lived miserable lives on over-crowded boats.

'What you've got to understand first of all,' said Thornley, drawing a deep breath, 'is that there's three different sorts of boatmen. There's ours and those that work for the other big companies running fly boats. Fly boats is usually men only. They work shifts, night and day, three to a boat – an' are properly supervised. Their families stay at home an' are better off than most. They work hard but we pay them well.'

He paused, looking hard at Best to see if he was taking all this in before continuing, 'Then there are the boats run by families – handed down like. Some of them keeps their craft very nice.'

Best and Emma had seen these gaily painted craft with their glinting brasswork on an outing to Brentford Lock one golden summer day when they were newly married. They hadn't had much time to ever become much more than newly married.

'But some of them don't keep them nice?' Best prompted.

'No, some is disgusting.'

'Same as on land.'

'That's right.' Thornley relaxed a little. He was on his home ground and there had been no accusatory questions about the loading of gunpowder.

'Then, there are the Rodney men – the casuals. A lot of them are nobbut idle loafers, doing a bit of work here and a bit there, getting drunk, having fights.'

'None of them would be working for you, of course?'

Thornley looked uneasy. In fact, there was a permanent feeling of unease about the man as though he was always expecting something unpleasant to happen. 'Well, not *all* the casuals are like that. Some are a lot better than others. Regular casuals you might say – an' our captains would take *these* sort on as crew.'

'There aren't really many boat people who can read and write, are there?'

'Well, no,' Thornley admitted. 'Most all of them is illiterate. That's why they can't never get off the boats. Mind you, some of them would like to read and write and they try to get their children taught a bit.'

Best had also heard that the boatmen had a reputation for stealing produce and game from the properties they passed through. But he felt there was not much point in bringing that up. Anyway, there wasn't that much harm in poaching from the rich, and generalizations, like those about ice-cream-selling, organ-playing Italians were likely to be true only in part.

'Many outsiders work the boats?' he asked instead. 'Railway navvies and the like?'

He shrugged. 'Scarce any. Even the Rodney men have usually grown up near the canal and, you know, done a bit of casual work on the water as kids; then, maybe, run away from home when they was lads. No, there's not many outsiders. Very tight bunch, canal folk.'

'What about the workmen in the yard?'

'Oh, them! Them's just your usual Londoners. You know, come from everywhere!' He laughed and instantly looked ten years younger.

'Paddies?'

'Yes, one or two. Let's see, our regulars are Mickie Rourke and Jamie O'Donnell – they've been here a few years. But there could be more among the casuals.'

'Any American Paddies around, are there?'

He looked puzzled again. Then it dawned. 'Oh, you're thinking of them Fenians. The others asked me that. Like I told them, never seen any – not that I know of that is.'

Best nodded ruefully. As he and his colleagues had already learned, these days not all Irish Americans made it easy for them with tell-tale accents or fancy clothes.

On his way out through the bustling yard, Best was halted by a shout, 'Hey, there!' A vaguely familiar figure approached with hand outstretched. It was George Grealey, the friendly and garrulous loader from the inquest.

Best was surprised that a company employee should be so openly friendly to a detective officer, given the circumstances, until he remembered that Grealey did not know he was a policeman.

'Been doing a bit of business?' The loader seemed proud to greet his dapper acquaintance, but abashed about proffering his grubby hand and made vain efforts to wipe it with a filthy handkerchief.

'A little,' Best grinned and tapped his nose conspiratorially. The loader's grip was painfully strong, all that lifting and humping doubtless. The shoulders, too, seemed more formidable now he was in shirt sleeves and he was perspiring heavily. 'Working hard, George?'

'Yeah,' he grinned, pleased that Best had remembered his name, but now that he was close up to that pristine presence, suddenly even more self-conscious about his appearance. He began dabbing ineffectively at his glistening face with the handkerchief and vainly straightening his neckerchief. 'I was just off for a break. Time for a smoke with me?'

They settled down on some boxes at the back of the yard and Best got in first to forestall any more questions about the 'business'. 'What are you loading this evening then, George?'

'Oh, same as always, mixed stuff. Always mixed stuff on the fly runs,' he explained, unwrapping a none-too-clean cloth bundle and taking out a large meat pie which he began hacking up with his clasp knife.

'Your boss keep you hard at it, does he?'

'Thornley? Nah, I never see 'im, do I?'

'No, I mean that other bloke. The miserable one sitting next to you at the inquest. Can't remember his name.' He could, it was Minchin, Joseph Minchin.

'Oh, 'im,' Grealey laughed, 'old Joe. Naw, 'e's all right really. Didn't like bein' there, that's all.' He proffered a piece of the pie.

'No thanks,' said Best with a regretful sigh. 'Just going for my supper. Daren't arrive without an appetite!'

Grealey grinned sympathetically at this typical picture of cosy domestic tyranny. 'Wise fellah.'

Sharing exasperation with the ways of the fair sex gave Best a lead-in. 'Joe sorted out his love-life yet?' he asked, casually.

Grealey laughed, 'Shouldn't think so!' At their inquest chat Grealey had confided that Minchin was trying to keep the sides of his love-triangle apart, but his ladyfriend was becoming difficult and the wife increasingly suspicious. The scenario was only too familiar. Best couldn't quite see the beaky, taciturn Minchin as the great lover, but you never could tell about these things.

'His scratches had nearly healed last time I saw him, though.'

When Grealey dropped this bombshell Best's head had been down, his gaze quietly contemplating the mud now clinging to his once glistening toe-caps. As the statement sank in, his head began to shoot up in response. He put the brakes on just in time, slowing the movement and wiping the startled look from his face, replacing it with one of polite interest.

'Got that bad, had it?'

'Not 'alf. Mary's a right fiery one, he says.'

'She the wife or the—?'

'Oh, the filly.'

They both laughed.

'Must say I don't remember seeing any scratches on him. Must have got them since I saw him.'

'Oh, no, he had them then. Down here.' Grealey drew his black-nailed index finger down his lower right cheek and neck. 'Tried to cover them up a bit with a scarf, but it weren't no good.'

Best had seen only the left cheek and the man had not turned his head. Damn, he should have persisted with Mr Minchin.

'Bit embarrassed, was he?'

'Yeah.' Grealey spluttered out flakes of pastry, 'Dunno why. I think it's something to be proud of – having two women fighting over you!'

With a show of reluctance Best took out his watch, looked suitably concerned at what it told him and said,

'Well, I'd better be going.' He stood up. 'Good to see you again.'

'Yeah – good to see you too.' Grealey began struggling with his cloth and pie as he tried get up but Best stayed him with an outstretched hand which turned into a friendly, farewell salute. One handshake had been above and beyond the call of duty. A second, with grease from the meat pie added, was more than could be expected.

'See you again.' He turned away, then as an afterthought said, 'Oh, is Minchin about, might as well have a word.'

'Oh no,' replied Grealey. 'Didn't you know, mate? He's gone.'

Chapter Six

'Gone!' exclaimed Cheadle. 'What the hell do you mean, *gone*?' Best had never seen him this angry.

'It's not as bad as it sounds, Chief Inspector.'

'Oh, is that right? A prime suspect departs from right under our noses and you tell me it's not so bad! Playing with words again, clever dick?'

Best refrained from mentioning that Minchin had only become a prime suspect by dint of his enquiries just before he learned of the man's departure. But he was angry with himself for not homing in on the man earlier. At least he would have seen the scratch marks. However, frantic enquiries with Thornley had established that Minchin had not disappeared into the unknown, merely grabbed the chance to earn a little extra money by replacing one of the still-injured boatmen on the fly run.

'He's due back in three days,' he pointed out. But they both knew that by the time he returned his scratches would have healed, the trail grown that bit colder and heaven knows what incriminating evidence disposed of on the journey.

'I could telegraph the local police and get them to stop him.'

'An' warn him he was under suspicion? Very bright idea.'

Best knew he was right. Please God the attraction of navvying on some obscure railway cutting was not beckoning the load-checker.

'You spoken to his wife?'

'No, I thought she might have some way of contacting him and warning him.'

'At least you did something right. Here,' – Cheadle thrust a thick file at him – 'Thames case, catch up on it. Might be some tie up.'

Best thought that would be a waste of time. The everlasting Thames case enquiry had been carried out by Inspector Sayer with Best's assistance some of the time and had got nowhere. 'Good idea, sir.'

The writing on the blue pages of the Detective Officer's Special Report began in the usual formal fashion:

I beg to report that, assisted by Sergeants Lansdowne and Best,
I have made enquiry respecting the portions of human body
found in the River Thames the particulars connected with which
are as follows:

Best gazed out of the window of the Sergeants' office on to Great Scotland Yard before reluctantly dragging himself back to the gruesome contents of the Thames case file. First came the details of the finding of the 'left upper quarter', then of the right upper quarter, then two 'sets of lungs'. One of these had been presented to Best by Inspector Marler of Thames Division who had found them floating under the second arch of Battersea Bridge. That had been a shock. They had thought they were dealing with only one body. But the second set of lungs did seem rather large. Indeed, they had later been found not to be human. Best spared himself the details as to how that conclusion had been drawn but could not avoid Inspector Sayer's gruesome postscript to his initial report:

Since writing the foregoing, the scalp and face of a woman
have been found on Dukeshore off Limehouse and, as this

portion appears to be the only one likely to afford any means
of identification (although slight), I would beg to suggest that
Dr Lemp be consulted as to the advisability of its being at once
placed in spirits.

At least he hadn't said pickled. Best already knew that had
been done and that in fact all the segments had been so
treated. Fortunately, the unpleasant duty of screening out
the morbidly interested from the genuinely concerned
members of the public come to view had been left to
Mr Haydn, the medical officer at the Clapham and
Wandsworth Workhouse. Also that Mr Hadyn had
arranged the segments in some semblance of human
order so that a photograph might be taken. A photograph
which, Best was all too painfully aware, was lying in wait
for him among the reports he had yet to read, and the
perusal of which, he was trying to persuade himself, was
unnecessary to the efficient dispatch of his duties.

But what really brought him up sharp was the fact that
the latest portions had been found at Limehouse. The
Limehouse Basin was where the Regent's Canal began
its journey. Ships entered the basin from the Thames, near
Dukeshore, and unloaded their goods on to various canal
boats. Admittedly, the *Tilbury*'s flotilla began its fateful
journey from further up the canal, at the City Road Basin,
but it was a connection nonetheless. Small but possibly vital.

The remains had been found scattered over a long
stretch of the Thames, running from Chelsea to Woolwich,
but Limehouse was right in the centre of that stretch –
and the remains could have been swept both ways by the
tides from that point.

Dr Lemp's report on the latest remains revealed that the
woman was about forty years of age, had short, dark hair
and eyebrows, a short, thick nose which was round at the
extremity, and somewhat large and coarse-looking ears

which had been pierced for earrings 'which have not been torn out'. Best knew that, had they been, robbery was a likely motive. This body could hardly be more different from their fair and fragile canal victim. The apparent cause of death was a blow to the temple from a blunt instrument.

Next in the file came a flurry of telegrams from Sayer and Best to the head of the Detective Branch. These reported on progress with various identification claims. First, a Mr Woods thought the remains could be those of his daughter, Eliza, a 25-year-old tailoress who had been seduced by her uncle before leaving home a year earlier. Sayer saw the uncle and was not impressed, deciding he was both untruthful and of unsavoury character. He had 'quiet observations' kept on the man, despite the fact that he thought Eliza probably too young to be the victim.

They telegraphed all divisions asking enquiries to be made at tailors' workshops. This had turned up two Adelaide Eliza Woods, one who had departed for America, and the other who was still working for a Mr Nash, Draper, High Street, Bromley in Kent. Mr Wood went down to Bromley and found that the second Adelaide Eliza Wood was not, in fact, his daughter and decided that the Eliza who had emigrated across the Atlantic did not sound like her either.

Just then, the master of Brunswick Wharf (where the right upper quarter had been found) called in at Clapham Police Station. He reported that a woman on a brick-carrying barge, which called in at his wharf, had told him that she was afraid of her cohabitee, a bargee, whom she thought was mad. Her description bore some resemblance to that of the victim. Best and Lansdowne had chased down the Thames to the barge's likely destinations, Rochester and Gravesend, only to be saluted at dawn by the supposed victim from the prow of her barge. Even the ebullient Best was crestfallen then.

And that had only been the beginning. A constant stream of claims followed, with relatives or friends in many cases becoming strangely insistent that, despite the body parts not having the requisite smallpox scars of the missing person, or the missing person not having the burn scars present on the remains, the remains must be those of their wife, their daughter or their lodger.

But all was not dross here for Best. He noted with excitement that among these odd people, some of whom he had dealt with, was another with a Limehouse connection, one of the missing women having lived with her husband in the area. She had been reported missing by a neighbour, but the husband had said the body was not hers. Sayer's enquiries were continuing on that one, even though the neighbour had also failed to identify the corpse.

The file also held the usual wad of letters from the public and newspaper cuttings both containing helpful suggestions for the police. For example, that the victim must be a lunatic escaped from an asylum, or a visiting foreigner and therefore not missed – possibly a Dutchwoman from one of their trading ships which came up the Thames. Or it was a medical student's jape.

The last, a popular theory, was robustly refuted by those in charge of bodies at hospital mortuaries and college dissection rooms. Dr Lemp's report put paid to that suggestion by declaring that the body parts had been *separated with a knife and saw, in an unscientific manner*, adding unequivocally, *The body has not been dissected for anatomical purposes, but has been cut up immediately after death. The vessels are quite empty*.

Eventually, as one of *The Times* cuttings reported, 'All the barge stories and many land stories have been investigated. The detectives,' the newspaper conceded, 'had enquired about numerous missing persons, some of whom had come from the most remote parts of the kingdom.'

They could say that again. No wonder Inspector Sayer had looked so tired and even Best's optimism faded. All their work had come to naught but contrary to Press reports, the Inspector was still doggedly searching, particularly for clothes. Now the waters had offered up another unidentified corpse of equally uncertain station in life.

'There are so *many* possibilities!' groaned Best as he gazed at the map of Britain's interlocking canal system which grew even denser as it reached the Midlands. 'She could have come from *anywhere* along here.' He swept his hand over the route taken by the fly boats as it straddled north-west across London then turned right to join the main arm of the Grand Junction near Uxbridge before heading north. At Northampton, the Grand Junction divided, one fork heading east to Leicester, and the other, north-west. 'Anywhere,' grumbled Best, 'Berkhamsted, Stoke Bruerne, Braunston – anywhere, anywhere.'

PC Smith nodded sympathetically. He had already learned to let Best have his little moments of despair without comment.

'Or she could have been pushed in at the spot where she was found in the Regent's Canal by one of the good citizens of St John's Wood or – or . . . ' Best flung down his pencil. If only they could identify her. If only she had a tattoo or a scar. How could it be so difficult? Someone must miss such a young woman by now?

He turned his attention to the fire insurance map. The City Road Basin was divided into neat boxes marked as timber yards, coal depots, iron works or miscellaneous warehouses. 'Thornley is right. She couldn't have boarded at City Road Wharf – it's so busy there.'

'She might not have been noticed among all the women from the family barges,' Smith offered.

Best shook his head firmly. 'Family boats don't load at the Grand Junction Company depot – which is here.' He ran his finger in a semi-circle encompassing the end of the basin. 'There are dozens of loading clerks, foremen, office workers, but only an occasional woman visitor. Bound to be noticed.' He hesitated then exclaimed, 'Unless of course,' – he smacked his hands together – 'unless of course she was dressed as a man!'

They looked at each other excitedly, then Smith's face fell.

'What?' demanded Best. 'Tell me.'

Smith grimaced. 'What about the petticoats?' He spread his hands apologetically. 'Could she have tucked those into trousers? I mean she might have . . . '

They both realized she couldn't have.

'Right,' said Best recovering fast. 'Other possibilities. Places she could have boarded between here and Regent's Park.' He pointed at the arrow denoting the first lock, 'I think we can safely disregard this one.'

'Too near the wharf?'

'Yes. Too many people about. Too busy. Too risky.' He went back to the map. 'Then we have this long tunnel.' His forefinger traced westwards across Islington and lost its way in the jumble of squared-off streets west of the Agricultural Hall.

They both gazed perplexedly at the map. Then Smith's sturdy finger plunged on to a spot just north of the Caledonian Road which marked the exit of Islington Tunnel. Best glanced back and forth from tunnel entrance to exit. 'That's an amazingly long tunnel?' He shook his head. 'The times I've walked through Islington and never realized that was underneath!' He paused to refocus on the map's tiny print, 'So, it looks as if the next likely spot is–'

'Battlebridge Basin,' they said in unison.

The Battlebridge Basin sliced a long oblong out of the south side of the canal, in the strange no-man's-land just beyond the tunnel and before North London's clutch of railway termini. Edging the basin were timber yards, a flour mill, an ice house, an iron foundry and some mixed merchandise warehouses and wharves. But the more Best and Smith looked at it, the more they realized that although it might look a likely spot it was an unlikely stopping place for a string of boats on a fast regular service to the Midlands, loaded up and just started on its run. Best shrugged and made another note in his list of new questions for the traffic manager: *Any reason to stop at Battlebridge Basin? Did they that night?*

It would help if he knew a bit more about the canals. But he had never needed to before. Canals were just there, somehow. Something one took for granted. You noticed them but somehow, strangely, you didn't. He'd seen the Islington Tunnel entrance before but had never thought about where the tunnel went or where the canal re-emerged.

'What we need to look at are the locks. It has to be a lock, I think. They have no choice but to stop there.'

The next stretch of canal curved into a long bend, fringed on the south side with a group of circles indicating the gasometers of the Imperial Gas Works. Then there was a series of straight lines where coal shutes led down to the water.

'Here's a lock.' Smith's finger plunged again to a boat-shaped island at the end of a long, unmarked sweep of canal. St Pancras double lock where, Thornley claimed, there had been a row between a man and a woman. Not only that, it was the site of the ugly writing on the wall. Behind it, open ground.

'Oh, this is interesting!' exclaimed Best. 'Very interesting!' They grinned at each other. They thought St Pancras double lock looked even more interesting when they discovered that the only *other* locks before the site of the explosion were the busy triple flight at Camden Town. He tapped his pencil abstractedly on the map. 'Of course, there is one other thing we haven't even considered ... '

Smith looked up enquiringly.

'She might not have been alive when she boarded. *If* she boarded that is.' He paused. Her body could have been wrapped in a roll of tarpaulin or carpet – or made into just another long parcel.'

Smith nodded. The thought sobered them both for a moment. What a sad end for a young girl, thought Best. Life is not fair. Nor death either. But then, he knew that already.

Something was nagging at Best. One of those thoughts which hover tantalizingly just out of reach. He concentrated, then, as it began to form, he tried to grab at it but it disappeared again. To distract himself, so that it might pop up unbidden, he turned his attention to the advertisements on the panel above the heads of the omnibus passengers opposite, but they were all too familiar: Oakey's Knife Polish, Gatti's Charing Cross Music Hall, Pears Soap and Holloway's Wonderful Pills for the Throat and Chest.

Much good Holloway's Wonderful Pills had done his Emma, he thought, bitterly. He knew that advertisement by heart – telling you that if you didn't take them 'at the commencement of a disorder, disastrous consequences would result'. Well, they had anyway. In fact, if she hadn't been taking Holloway's Wonderful Pills she might have gone to the doctor sooner.

The fearful expression on the face of the young woman opposite brought Best up sharp. He realized he was glaring ferociously. She must think him mad. Slowly he relaxed his face until it took on an almost benign expression then switched his gaze to a more cheerful advertisement, that for Gatti's Music Hall. Happier memories there. Emma loved Gatti's ice-cream, both the penny-licks and the striped hokey-pokeys. And Gatti's Palace of Varieties had been a familiar haunt for him and his colleagues when they lived at the single man's section house in Westminster.

Now, there was an Italian immigrant who had done well for himself – Carlo Gatti. He had arrived in London from Switzerland, practically penniless, and had gone out into the streets to sell coffee and roast chestnuts, begun the craze for the penny-lick ice-creams and ended up owning restaurants, billiard halls and music halls. The Gattis were also London's biggest ice suppliers. When he was on the beat Best had often chatted to the drivers of their black and yellow carts as they did their rounds to restaurants, shops and houses of the wealthy, dropping off huge slabs of frozen water.

'Ice!' Best exclaimed suddenly. 'That's it! Ice!'

Chapter Seven

Best now had the full attention of all the passengers, not just the frightened young woman opposite. But he didn't care. Ice! Smiling idiotically, the Sergeant jumped vigorously to his feet, causing the omnibus to sway and the conductor to look cross.

He was still feeling pleased with himself when he alighted from a second omnibus at the end of the Caledonian Road. Stepping lightly, he took the first left into Wharfdale Road, then right into New Wharf Road which backed on to the Battlebridge Basin. The day was bright and sunny but there was a tingle in the air and a mistiness in the distance. Autumn behaving as it should, at last. Perhaps it was a sign. He passed a flour mill and there it was – a three-storey, yellow-brick building with red brick trim. Writ large above the arched entrance: Carlo Gatti, Ice Merchant.

The archway led into an interior yard where Best turned in, squeezing his way alongside one of the familiar, high-sided carts and deliberately resisting the urge to look up at the two huge, sweating horses towering above him.

The company office was like most warehouse offices – a partitioned oblong with half-windowed walls which allowed a good view of the activity going on in the yard outside. The man in charge, one Carlo Offridi, was a short, solid-looking man in his thirties who had little English – and what he did have he seemed reluctant to utilize on Best. Only after the Sergeant had switched to Italian, discovered some mutual aquaintances in the community, assured the man that he wanted only to know a little about ice selling to assist him with some cases of fraud involving a competitor, did Offridi begin to relax and show him around.

In the yard by the far wall which overlooked the canal basin were two brick-lined ice wells, like giant pudding basins buried in the earth.

'They hold five tons each,' offered Carlo, obviously warmed by Best's wonder. Best found the sight of two workmen sitting down among the ice blocks drinking tea even more amazing.

'It's hard work,' said Offridi, misunderstanding Best's startled glance, 'they need to stop here and there.'

Carlo was soon called upon to check a disputed load so he deposited Best back in the office where Jones, the English clerk, gave him a cup of coffee before retreating behind his ledgers. Best did not intend to let him stay there. He guessed, by the man's deference that he had judged him to be some prospective customer from a foreign restaurant.

'Is it true,' Best enquired of him, 'that some of the ice comes all the way from Norway?' It sounded like just curiosity but it was more than that. Best really wanted to know everything about this ice-transportation business.

'All of it,' nodded Jones politely.

'Remarkable,' Best shook his head. 'And how long does that take?'

'About six days,' Jones laughed, 'with the wind in the right direction, 'course.'

'But why doesn't the ice melt?'

'Oh, it does, some of it, dunnit? About a third, usually. But,' he grinned, 'we only pays for what's left. It gets measured as it comes in – down at Limehouse Dock.'

'Amazing,' exclaimed Best, 'amazing.'

Having amazed Best once, Jones was eager to do so again. A pale little man with a pale little life he didn't often get to become the centre of attention.

'Some companies gets it from America, you know. But we never have. Used to take some from the canal when it froze over, way back that was. But you couldn't be sure of gettin' it an' it was pretty dirty when you did. You should have seen some of the things we found in it!'

Best thought he would rather not know and got him back on track with, 'So now it all comes from Norway?'

The man was warming to his theme now, ' Oh, yeah!' he said excitedly. 'Got great lakes of it there, they have, so you can cut it in thick slabs, regular size an' all. Then it grows again, they say, an' they get another load from the same place!'

Best had never heard of ice 'growing'. He shook his head. 'Fascinating,' and he meant it.

Jones took Best's eagerness as a tribute to his own, hitherto unappreciated, scintillating personality so that when Best asked, 'How often do shipments come in?' he couldn't wait to scintillate again.

Ice shipments came in only from spring to October he revealed. In the winter, the Norwegian boats got iced in which Best and Jones found very droll. More to the point, the last shipments had arrived a week earlier. It occurred to Best that what had come in last would be used first as the pit filled up. He must keep that in mind.

'Colourful fellows, are they? These Norwegians?' Maybe the fair victim had come from Scandinavia.

'Dunno. We never sees them – just the canal boatmen, that's all we ever sees.' He grimaced at his new friend, to indicate his low opinion of the latter.

Offridi returned, clipboard in hand and a preoccupied look on his face. Best decided not to outstay his welcome. The rather relieved foreman held up his clipboard apologetically and motioned to the clerk to accompany the visitor off the premises.

The yard was frantic now and the noise deafening. The rattle of harness and heavy wheels on cobblestones competing against the grinding and rattle of the cranes as they reached down into the wells for their glistening burdens.

'They must be strong to do that!' shouted Best, as he dodged out of the path of a man pushing and guiding the slabs on to his cart.

'They're used to it,' shrugged Jones.

He couldn't see any stables. 'Where do you keep all the horses?' asked Best, as he pressed himself against a wall to avoid a handsome pair of dark-brown drays with white flashes on their noses.

Jones jerked his head upwards. 'Stables are up there.' He pointed to where a fairly steep path led up to the first floor. They were almost at the entrance when, without having to probe any further, Jones offered Best the information he was seeking.

'The grooms and some of the ice-men live up there, as well. Only the single ones, of course.'

They shook hands in a friendly, nonchalant fashion and Best strolled off again down New Wharf Road. The sun was less bright now but his heart was even lighter. Cheadle had asked him to find 'somewhere cool' and he had found it. Not only that, it was on the canalside. All he had to do was work out how the body had got to Regent's Park. An ice cart! Or – he remembered something Jones had said – of course, that was it!

'The body could have been put in the ice well two weeks before the explosion,' an excited Best explained to a doubting Cheadle and a startled Smith' – wrapped in sacking, or similar – until the murderer – maybe one of the ice-men or a groom – saw his chance to get rid of her. Just his bad luck it should be on the night of the explosion.'

There was a short, surprised silence before Cheadle murmured drily, 'All a bit too fanciful, if you ask me.

I mean, it's heavy stuff, that ice, wouldn't it crush the body?'

Best hadn't thought of that. 'It's only one possibility, sir,' he said defensively. 'I'm only trying every picture, like you said. Liza Moody lived quite near the canal. She's the nearest match we've got so far – and you did say the body might have been kept somewhere cool . . . '

'All right, all right,' the Chief Inspector answered, shooting himself up in his chair and causing Smith, who had never seen this pantomime before, to almost jump out of his own seat in surprise. 'Just supposing you're right,' Cheadle said, in a more placatory tone, 'how d'you suppose the body got to Regent's Park?'

'Easily,' said Best, playing his trump card. 'Ice doesn't just get unloaded from boats at Battlebridge – it gets loaded up – to go north.'

'Hmph. Well, we'll see. You think that makes more sense if the victim is this barmaid, Eliza Moody?'

'It's only ten minutes' walk away.'

'What did you find out at the Three Tuns, young Smith?'

'Well, the landlord now thinks she did just go off of her own accord.'

'That right?' murmured Cheadle quietly. 'And did he say what made him think that?'

'Yes,' said Smith eagerly. 'At first he thought she had no followers, but now he remembers there was a man who was thick with her, a dark bloke with a scar on his lip – dressed like a sailor.'

Cheadle and Best looked at each other.

'Sir?' said Smith, reddening.

'Anything else?'

'Yes.' He looked from one to the other uncertainly. 'At first he thought there was nothing missing, but some money had gone after all . . . '

'A man gifted with afterthought,' murmured Best.

'He was doing his books and he just noticed . . . '

Cheadle and Best were getting to their feet. 'I'll get the cab', said Best.

'He's a very pleasant man, easy-going,' exclaimed Smith, adding desperately, 'much too fat to attack anyone . . . ' He had been going to go on to say something about Maisie and how she was about to tell him something and how he had been unable to find her again, but thought this did not seem a good moment.

The Yard men were too late. By the time they arrived at the Three Tuns the area was thick with policemen. Liza Moody had been found. The smell met them at the top of the cellar steps. Below, her remains lay half out on the stone floor and half remaining in the barrel which had contained the body. Everything was so soggy and decomposing that it might have been hard to tell what had happened to her had it not been clear by the grotesquely lolling head that her throat had been cut. Alongside, another body. This time, male. Its wiry form had fallen almost into an S shape after being cut down from the noose suspended from a hoisting hook in the ceiling. The remains of dark ale from the broken barrel had stained the dead man's rough tweed trousers, rolled-up sleeves and tow-coloured hair.

'I had no notion at all, no notion,' said an emotional Welsh voice, as the landlord came up behind the detectives. 'My cellarman for ten years he was, and I did not even notice his passion for young Liza. Maisie came to me and said he had been bothering the girl, I asked him about it – and this is how it all ends!' He shook his head. The voice had risen, the face remained impassive, but there was a tear in the eye.

It seemed, then, that the case was already solved. A murder followed by a suicide due to remorse, or for fear of being caught. Nonetheless, a full investigation would have to take place. Someone, after all, may have assisted the barman on to the hook. If that were so, who else might now be in danger? Maisie, in case she changed her story? Best wondered who would get the docket for this one. Thank goodness it wouldn't be him.

Before the unscheduled rush to Somers Town, Best had planned to go to St John's Wood to see Van Ellen again, or down to City Road to chase up any news on Minchin.

Cheadle knocked both ideas on the head by waving a bundle of letters in his face. 'The latest arrivals – the commissioner wants them looked at and actioned immediately. See to it, will you?'

Best sighed inwardly. He hated this duty. Everyone knew better than the Detective Branch, had a better theory or some wonderful information to impart. He wondered if they ever realized how the extra burden of their letters lessened the detectives' chances of finding the murderer. Of course, he had to admit that, occasionally, they did turn up something useful, but not often. With these bitter thoughts on his mind he retired to the Sergeants' room, clutching his bundle of time-wasters.

Best gave the pile of letters a quick run through to weed out the mad ones. The first was written in a large, sprawling hand on a ridiculously small piece of paper so that it amounted to no more than two sentences. The second was in miniscule writing, edge-to-edge on a large piece of watermarked vellum. The writing on the next started out even, controlled and of normal size but soon grew larger and larger and began leaping off in every direction. The text was embellished by huge capital letters and rows of angry exclamation marks: a mad one. The contents, he knew, would be depressingly familiar. The writer would have some secret knowledge he wished to pass on to the police. It was being divulged only to him via the new

Electric Telegraph which seeped through his bedroom walls, or by some spirit forms materializing before him, but he was being pursued by evil people out to thwart him or even destroy him. The Sergeant put two mad letters to one side, lit the office lamps, took out his cigarettes and began to work his way through the rest, making notes as he went.

A woman in Bow had a neighbour whose husband was always threatening to kill her – and she hadn't seen her for two weeks. A gentleman writing from his club in St James's wanted to know why they hadn't rounded up all the suspected Fenians as the explosion was obviously their work. Another gentleman had seen a pretty young girl walking towards Macclesfield Bridge on the evening before the explosion. A woman in Holland Park had just returned home from a trip abroad to find her young sister was missing and had reported it to the police who seemed to be doing nothing. A semi-literate person, who preferred to remain anonymous, actually named the murderer as one of the evangelists trying to save the souls of the narrow-boatmen. The writer suggested that, should police care to drag the canal from the Paddington Basin to Brent, they would find many more such bodies. And so on.

The missing women from Bow and Holland Park seemed to be the most promising so he set to work on those making notes for the Clerk Sergeant to copy in his fine script for the replies. He had barely begun when a messenger popped his head around the door.

'There's a woman downstairs wanting to see someone working on the canal murder – something about a missing sister. She looks angry.'

That took the biscuit, thought Best. 'She's not the only one!' he exploded, banging down one of the letters. 'I'm sick of people wasting my time. I'm angry too!' He got up and stamped out, causing his colleague to smile after him affectionately. That foreign blood again.

Chapter Eight

Best strode into the interview-room. His irritation at the interruption propelled him forward too fast, startling the small, neatly dressed woman sitting by the bare wooden table. Their eyes met, his impatient, hers puzzled.

'I'm Sergeant Best,' he snapped out more sharply than he intended. 'What can I do to help you, Mrs–'

She stiffened 'And I'm *Miss* Franks,' she replied coldly. 'Miss Helen Franks. But then if you had read my letter you would have known that, *wouldn't you?*'

'We receive a great many letters, Miss Franks,' he retorted, still trying to get his brakes to grip properly, 'and I must tell you that we are extremely busy trying to solve this murder.'

'All the more reason, I suggest, that you read your post. The answer might be contained within.'

'That's very doubtful!' They glared at each other. 'I assure you, Miss Franks,' he went on, with some venom, 'that Scotland Yard's post is read very thoroughly, your letter included.'

It was dawning on him that this must be the woman from, Holland Park whose sister was missing. Probably one of those ladies of leisure who had nothing to do but contemplate her own affairs. 'May I suggest that because nothing is seen to have been done, you need not presume that nothing has been!'

An icy silence reigned between them. Best knew he had probably gone too far and she might have influential friends who would complain to the commissioner, but sometimes he couldn't help himself. This impasse was ridiculous, though, and unprofessional. He was about to utter a more placatory phrase when she beat him to it by saying in a still firm but less hostile tone, 'I can see that you are harassed, Sergeant, so I will make allowances. But you must understand that I am extremely worried about my sister and need your help.'

Best held up his hand in a manner of half capitulation and inclined his head further, to suggest a truce. He was not a petty man. 'Of course. I will do all I can.' He sat down opposite her, took out his notepad and pencil and said, 'Right, Miss Franks, tell me about your sister.'

'I'd better tell you about both of us,' she replied, looking him directly in the eye in a manner unusual for a woman, 'then you will be able to grasp the whole picture.' She paused for a moment to gather her thoughts then began, 'My sister, Matilda, is nineteen years old. We live together in a small house in Holland Park. Our parents are dead.' Extending her hand slightly to ward off sympathetic noises she went on dispassionately, 'And whilst we are fortunate that my father left few debts, he left us very little money either. Thus, we two ladies, educated to expect a life of relative leisure, are obliged to work.' She gave him a sharp look. 'I assure you that that is not an idea which disturbs me, Mr Best. In fact, I would welcome it, were employment opportunities for women similar to those for men.'

She was no beauty, thought Best, but her features were pleasant enough. He wondered why she had never married, she must be at least thirty.

'But fate has smiled on me in one respect,' she went on. 'Like many women of leisure I studied art when I was younger, and found I had a certain facility. Since I had no wish to become a governess,' – she spat out the word – 'I took up art again after father's death – in the hope of gaining some financial return.'

She was one of those women artists! The idea excited Best. Even the *Graphic* published drawings by women, occasionally. You certainly got to meet all kinds of people in this job. But why was she so prim and pedantic? Artists were supposed to be free spirits.

'I have been moderately successful, despite the fact–' She stopped herself. 'Oh, never mind that – too far from the point. Suffice to say that women are not allowed to attend life classes in London, but can do so in Paris. As I needed the experience, I went there – five weeks ago.'

'And your sister?'

She gave him a bleak look. 'My sister stayed here.'

There was a short silence which she ended by continuing, 'Our limited means prevented both of us going and she had plenty to do selling my pictures.'

Best couldn't hide his surprise. 'She goes around alone, selling your pictures?'

'Good heavens, no. She always takes our housekeeper or a relative with her. She has no skills, you see, but is very pretty, and this can be a great advantage in selling pictures to gallery owners who are, of course, all men. She was very shy at first. But, since my father died, we have both had to make sacrifices and accept challenges. I am very proud of her.'

Best's spirits were rising again. They had an art connection!

'Do you know St John's Wood?'

'Of course.' Her eyes lit up and, for the first time, her response was spontaneous. 'The Land of the Artists!'

'Do you know anyone there?'

She nodded. 'Several people – and I took lessons from Lawrence Alma-Tadema and his wife. Not quite my style, but useful experience nonetheless. She's the better artist, I think, but–' She pulled herself up again.

'Did Matilda ever go there?'

'No. At least I don't think so.' She looked anxious. 'I can't remember her doing so . . . '

'Don't worry about it, Miss Franks. If she did, I'm sure it will come to you later. Now, when did she go missing?'

Tears started into her grey eyes. 'That's just it. I don't know. I wasn't here. But it seems as though . . .' – she found it difficult to get the next bit out – 'as though it was the day before the canal explosion!' Now, the tears were unstoppable. She groped about in her leather satchel for a handkerchief. Best gave her the immaculate folded one from his breast pocket. 'This is ridiculous,' she said, angrily, 'and helps no one.'

'It's only human, Miss Franks,' he said gently. 'And it does help me to accept that you are genuine.'

She choked. 'Genuine! Good God, man, you are not telling me that people make this kind of thing up!'

He nodded. 'Makes them feel important. Gets them attention.'

She gazed at him in astonishment. 'Unbelievable!'

'But do go on. Tell me what your sister looked like.'

'I've brought a photograph.' She fished in a large, plush handbag. 'It was taken two years ago but . . . ' She held it out to him.

He stopped her, 'You do realize that the victim's face was very badly disfigured?'

'I didn't, no. No, I didn't know that.' She was stumbling. 'But surely. . . ?'

He shook his head. 'I'm afraid not. I'll look at it of course but . . . '

She pushed it into his hand. The setting was commonplace: potted plant on plinth, draped curtains. The pose equally so. Young girl in her Sunday best, shy but proud. Matilda was obviously fair, like the victim, young and slight also but he really had no idea whether it was the same young woman that he had last seen decomposing on the mortuary slab at St Marylebone Workhouse. He shook his head again. 'I don't know.'

'There must be something?'

'Had she any marks, scars?'

'On her left cheek – a mole.'

He shook his head again.

'The girl's cheek was too disfigured?' She forced out the words as she contemplated the horror of them.

He filled the silence quickly. 'Have you any idea what she was wearing?'

'The only clothing that I can be certain is missing is a pale-blue ensemble.' She smiled suddenly. 'She looked so pretty in that. It showed off her colouring and . . . what's the matter?'

'Nothing.' Best cursed himself, he must try to keep more control on his expression.

'There is – but there was nothing in the notice about the victim wearing a blue dress.'

'You're right. But, I must be honest.' Too late to be anything else, he thought. 'It's just that among the letters I was reading when you arrived, is one about a pretty young lady in a pale-blue dress. Wait here.'

He returned with the letter and they read it together. On a folded, upright oblong of paper headed with a cryptic, *Carlton, St James's*, it began, *My dear Henderson*. In typically careless, aristocratic scrawl, it went on, *I happened to be in Regent's Park the night before the explosion. Saw a damned pretty girl in light blue hurrying towards Macclesfield Bridge. Like woman found in canal had fair hair and pale skin. Worth looking into? I shall be at home and available tomorrow evening and the next between 6 and 8 p.m.*

The almost illegible signature looked like 'Maitland' or 'Mallard' and the address scrawled below read *Hill Hse, Randolph Avenue, Maida Vale*.

As she read the letter, Helen Franks grew paler. 'The night before the explosion,' she murmured as she read, 'near the bridge!'

'Doesn't mean it *was* her,' said Best. 'The links are still tenuous.'

She was not comforted and he did not blame her. Time for some decisive action. He checked the date on the letter. Yesterday. 'What I think we need to do straight away,' he said firmly, surprising himself with his resolution as he did sometimes, 'is to go to see this gentleman and get some more details.' He stood up.

'What, now?'

'Yes, now.'

'Both of us?'

'Yes, unless you have some other plans?'

'The only plan I have, Mr Best,' she replied, some of the crispness returning to her voice, 'is to find my sister. Nothing else matters.' She stood up. He was touched to see how tiny she was and yet, how resolute.

'Good. On the way, you can tell me more about Matilda.'

The omnibus would be too slow and inappropriate, in the circumstances, thought Best as he helped Miss Franks into one of the cabs waiting on the rank conveniently situated within Great Scotland Yard. He hoped the commissioner would see it that way when it came to agreeing his expenses. The fog, which had been just a misty hint in the air was now thickening, blotting out the usual view of Horse Guards Parade seen through the Yard's entrance. Best had quite liked London fogs, within limits. Like snow, they changed the everyday world into something new. But he had begun to feel differently when he saw what that murky air did to Emma. Now, he thought, as he turned his attention back to Helen Franks, it at least did away with the distraction of the passing scene.

'So, when did you last hear from your sister, Miss Franks?'

'Three weeks ago.'

'And everything seemed in order?'

'Perfectly. Very good, in fact. It was a light-hearted letter. She had just sold two of my paintings.'

'How did you discover she was missing, and when?'

'My cousin, Jane, wrote to me. Matilda had left home, on what I now know was the afternoon before the explosion. Mrs Briggs, our housekeeper, was surprised when she didn't come back that evening but thought she must have gone to see our cousins in Pinner and had decided to stay the night – as she often did. When she didn't return the following day, Mrs Briggs presumed that she must be staying with them for a few days. It's not like Matilda to go off without telling anyone but, in fact, she had told Mrs Briggs that she intended to stay at Pinner for a few days the following week. Mrs Briggs thought she must have got the dates wrong. She's getting on and is inclined to be forgetful, and knows it, poor dear.

'After a week, and still no word, she began to get really worried and went to see the cousins. She discovered that they had not seen Matilda since well before the afternoon in question. They contacted other relatives and friends, none of whom knew of Matilda's whereabouts. Then they telegraphed me. I came home at once. That was four days ago.'

They had reached Edgware Road, that long straight avenue which continues almost due north until it becomes Maida Vale. The high buildings, offices and shops acted like a long tunnel the walls of which echoed their slow, clip-clopping progress. In this brief respite between home-going and theatre-going there was little other traffic around for company. The fog began to lift slightly as they proceeded north and their speed increased in consequence.

'Tell me more about your sister, her appearance and character.'

'Well, she is very sheltered and quite shy but, as I said, showed her mettle when it mattered. She's still very naïve, though, and needs protecting.'

'Yet you went away.'

'Mr Best, I had no choice!' she rejoined angrily. 'It was essential that I improved my technique and kept up or I would not have been able to continue to earn my living – meagre though it is – and we would both have starved.'

Or become governesses, he thought. He suddenly realized why her gaze was so disconcerting. She did not care what he thought of her, was unconcerned whether he liked her or not. She made no attempt to please. He wasn't accustomed to that in women, other than the aristocratic types with whom he sometimes came in contact through his work, and even they, as he was not an unattractive man . . .

'Did your sister have anything to do with artists?'

'No,' Helen Franks replied, almost too quickly. But Best did not notice. He was tired and hungry and his head was spinning. From a position of having no likely identity for his victim he now seemed to have an embarrassment of contenders for the post: boatman's doxy, girl in blue, and now Matilda Franks.

He would like to have closed his eyes and dozed the rest of the way, but the enforced intimacy of the hansom disallowed that. Besides which, because she was so obviously resistant to his charms, he felt a sudden impulse to impress Helen Franks with his artistic knowledge. His effort, however, came out as a rather trite; 'I do admire Rose Bonheur.'

'Really?' she replied coldly. 'I think you will find you are not alone there. She is, after all, the acceptable woman artist.'

Feeling squashed, Best snapped back, 'Well, that doesn't mean she is not a good artist, does it?'

They glared at each other again before each turned away to look out of the windows, just as the cab slowed down and began the turn from Maida Vale towards Randolph Avenue. Who cared about the opinion of this drab and shrewish spinster, with the scorpion in her tail? Best thought sourly. Any very ordinary Italian woman would easily put her in the shade. Her missing sister might be a Nordic goddess, but she was an English mouse and did not deserve his attention.

Like its owner, Sir Giles Maitland, the drawing-room of Hill House was florid. Crimson velvet upholstery, panels of crimson-flock wallpaper and the glint of gilt trim everywhere – from the Louis-Quinze furniture to the mouldings on the stucco ceiling. The whole effect, decided Best, was pleasantly opulent.

Sir Giles Maitland's cheeks also tended towards crimson in places. A stout, heavily moustached gentleman in his early sixties, he had welcomed them courteously, particularly Helen with whom he adopted exaggerated gallantry. Her response, Best was interested to note, was cool but polite. Despite being clearly disappointed by Best's modest rank (when police callers were announced he had expected, at least, a Chief Inspector) Sir Giles was, nonetheless, rather tickled with his role in the mystery.

He studied the photograph carefully before admitting, 'Honestly, m'dear, I could not say . . . ' Indeed, his memory of the girl in blue seemed to be restricted to the facts that she wore blue and was dashed pretty – which got them no further forward.

Helen Franks responded by simplifying the details of ladies' attire into language which a mere male might understand. Maitland concentrated hard as she asked him whether the dress material had been flimsy with little spots? Had he noticed any velvet trimmings? Was some part of the ensemble, such as the wrap and the flounces at the bottom of the skirt, a deeper blue than the rest? He could remember none of these things. All he knew was that, though slight, the girl had a fine figure which could be glimpsed as her wrap flew out as she walked, and that she was as fair as an ice-maiden and had a froth of curls on her forehead.

'Her hat? Don't remember, sorry. Small, I think – oh, and it had something hanging forward.' He raised his hand to describe a curve out and over his forehead. 'Not feathers, I don't think . . . '

'Forget-me-nots,' said Helen Franks quietly.

'That's it! Forget-me-nots!' Sir Giles was delighted to get something right – until he saw the expression on Helen's face. 'Oh, my dear lady, I'm so sorry.' He rushed forward to grasp her hand. 'I did wonder,' he burbled, 'what such a pretty girl was doing out on her own in the park. I mean, she looked so respectable . . . '

'She *was. Is*,' rejoined Helen firmly.

'Of course, m'dear. Of course.'

'Was she carrying anything?' broke in Best.

'A parasol, as I said,' he murmured, relieved to change the subject. 'Blue, of course,' he added shrugging apologetically.

There was a short silence, broken by an exclamation from Sir Giles. 'I remember! I remember! She had a small bag. A carpet bag. It was out of place with such a dainty outfit. It was in dark green. That's it! Just a minute, just a minute!' He was trying to grasp at the elusive memory. He closed his eyes and held one hand out to stop their questions, putting the other to his forehead to aid his concentration. The stance might have looked comically dramatic in less serious circumstances. 'Not just green, not just green,' he struggled. 'Got it! Not just green,' – his eyes flew open – 'check, kind of checks.'

Helen began to speak, but he silenced her again as he struggled for more. The only sound came from the ticking of the magnificent ormolu and turquoise porcelain clock on the mantelpiece behind him. 'Plaid, that's it,' he said finally and with some relief. 'Green, black and blue plaid, just like—'

'The Black Watch tartan,' finished Helen softly.

They stared at each other.

'That's right m'dear,' Sir Giles confirmed kindly, 'just like the Black Watch tartan.'

'But what was she *doing* there!' Helen burst out. 'I can't think what she could be *doing* there!'

Best got up. It seemed a good time to move. 'We will do our best to find out,' he said resolutely. 'Our very best. Now, let me take you home.'

'There was a flash above the *Tilbury's* cabin and a short report – like the sound of a gun – the sort of gun you would use to shoot sparrows,' said White who had been the labourer on the Dee when she sank. 'Then came some shouting.'

The man was a pathetic sight. The severity of his injuries had kept him from the earlier inquest hearings. Now, between his slow and hesitant answers, his lips kept moving as he mumbled quietly to himself. But, for the jury's benefit, he managed to relive the loading-up at City Road, the waiting until the little fleet was assembled, then the procession up the canal to the explosion point.

After that, he remembered nothing. Yes, he knew there had been a second explosion but he didn't remember what it was like. No, he didn't recall any smoke.

There was a murmur of interest when the next witness appeared. Being the country's leading poisons expert he was a familiar figure at sensational murder inquests and trials. This time, however, the tall and imposing Professor Alfred Swaine Taylor was demonstrating his expertise in the causes of explosions and the dangers of naphthalene storage. But he was also a victim/witness, for his house at 15 St John's Wood Terrace had been among those badly damaged by the explosion.

It was one of the many strange coincidences, Best reflected, in what was turning out to be a very strange case. He had never known one which had involved so many well-known personages as well as such a strange assortment of people: artists and scientists, businessmen and boatmen, rich and poor, the famous and the obscure.

Professor Taylor informed the coroner that he had seen many boats and steam tugs pass his house at all hours of the day and night.

He then added, somewhat dramatically for such an experienced professional witness, 'On winter nights I have seen a fiery tug going along like a luminous meteor among the trees – sparks going in all directions.'

Either living among artists or becoming a victim for a change was having an adverse effect on him. Perhaps both. He reverted to being the more matter-of-fact expert when he explained that the sparks could carry as far as forty to fifty yards – when the wind was blowing hard. And, as to the cause of the tragedy, the now ageing professor demonstrated that he had lost none of his scientific certainty. The benzoline carried on board had been the catalyst.

'Benzoline is exceedingly inflammable and highly volatile,' he explained. 'The problem is the vapour which pours off the oil – only a glass container, tightly stoppered, will hold it. It would seep through anything else such as wood,' he assured the jury. The benzoline carried by the *Tilbury* had been contained in wooden barrels.

'In normal circumstances,' Taylor continued, 'the vapour would disperse but, in this case, it accumulated slowly under the tarpaulin becoming "fearfully dense".

Anything red-hot would have inflamed it – a cinder from a chimney, or more especially, a naked flame. The tarpaulin would probably have protected it from sparks from above, but the tarpaulin had also served as a tunnel. When the cabin fire drew air towards it, as all fires do, it also drew (through the sight hole in the bulkhead) the deadly gas – and ignited it. *That* was the cause of the fire, *and* the subsequent explosion.'

The jury looked relieved at such calm, expert conviction after a mass of seemingly unconnected, circumstantial evidence and speculation.

The noises White had heard tied in with the professor's hypothesis.

'A gaseous explosion is short and sharp in its report,' he explained in answer to a juryman's question. *That* accounted for the early gunshot bang. 'Gunpowder is a little slower to go off and needs to be heated to five hundred and forty degrees.' That accounted for the second explosion. 'In my opinion,' the professor concluded, 'the accident would never have happened had benzoline not been carried or had the cabin been lighted only by a Davy safety lamp.'

The Home Office explosives expert not only agreed that the tunnel of benzoline must have been ignited by the cabin fire and the gunpowder explosion caused by that fire flashing back over the load – he demonstrated the theory in spectacular fashion. Into the bows of a scale model of a canal boat he poured half an inch of liquid benzoline, then he covered the cargo with tin (to represent tarpaulin) and touched the cabin area with a lighted taper. There was an immediate loud report and a rush of flame down the length of the boat.

The jury gasped. They had not been quite so awake since the start of the proceedings nearly three weeks earlier.

Well, at least that was an answer to one question, thought Best, and it knocked the Fenians and the rival railways out of the picture, or at least pushed them way down near the bottom of the list. Of course, experts could be wrong. Despite his air of implacable confidence, Professor Taylor's expertise had occasionally been challenged and found wanting – as the police knew to their cost when one of his errors had brought about the reprieve and release of convicted murderer, Dr Smethurst.

An even more pathetic figure than White appeared to give the answer to another burning question. A feeble old man from the village of Brades, near Birmingham, identified the third corpse as that of his nineteen-year-old son who had left home a year earlier. A tactful chat with the old man before the hearing had convinced Best that the old man would be of little help in establishing his son's relationships with women.

Finally, Sergeant Best was called upon to give a report on the progress, or lack of it, regarding the identification of the woman. He had to admit there had been little so far. In answer to questions from the coroner, he reminded the jury that it was thought her body had not been in the canal for long, there being little sign that various water-borne creatures had begun to feed on the body.

The jury brought in a verdict of accidental death on the boatmen and the coroner postponed the inquest on the female victim until such time as some progress had been made. When that happened, Best had no doubt that it would be Chief Inspector Cheadle who would be standing where he was now.

Chapter Nine

A terrible guilt was weighing on Mrs Briggs, the Franks's housekeeper. She had not realized that Matilda was missing as early as she might have done and, not knowing, had not informed anyone. Trying to convince her that it may not have made any difference proved a futile task. Best was grateful that the woman was sensible enough to dry her tears so as to answer his questions.

'You see, I knew she was going to Pinner for a few days while Helen was away and when she didn't come back that evening,' she said, dabbing at the corners of her pale-blue eyes, 'I just thought that's where she was.'

'Wouldn't she have reminded you before she went?'

'Usually, yes. But,' she added apologetically, 'I might not have remembered.'

Before leaving them together in her front parlour, Helen had spoken to her cook-housekeeper almost as though to a friend or relative. Best followed suit, but in the rather firmer tone necessary for sharpening witnesses' responses and making them think carefully about their replies. In most social exchanges answers tend to be tempered so as not to upset anyone, so half-truths reign. He wanted the full truth. Not easy to extricate from servants when it came to their employers.

'You're a little forgetful?'

To his surprise she blushed and said, 'Yes, well, maybe . . .'

He was intrigued. A typical, plump, middle-aged cook-housekeeper of unremarkable appearance, she had a certain extra something Best found it hard to put his finger on.

'Go on. Maybe . . . what?'

She was silent for a moment, contemplating her short fingernails, then said in a rush, 'You see, I might never have heard.'

'You're a little deaf, then?' he nodded, understandingly.

'Oh no, not really.' She stopped again, looked down again at her surprisingly neat little hands then straight up at him. 'I know they think I'm forgetful or deaf.' She gave him a quick, conspiratorial smile. 'But, honest truth, I don't always listen to them.'

Best wanted to laugh but managed to suppress his mirth. The indefinable something was intelligence and humour. Teach him to make assumptions.

'Not on purpose, do you see?' she went on. 'It's just that sometimes the girls tell me things when I'm busy – fitting the pastry crust on to a pie or polishing an awkward bit of the grate. Sometimes they might be telling me about things I don't really understand, or I might be thinking of something else – like you do when you're doing boring things, you know?'

Best nodded. 'Very understandable.' He suspected that 'the girls', despite their straitened circumstances, had little experience of doing anything really boring.

'So I just nod and say something like, "Oh, yes? Is that right? You don't say so?"'

She reminded him of his mother – keeping them all happy while working herself into an early grave. They always called her forgetful when she failed to recall a vital event in their small lives, but he couldn't ever remember being required to listen to her problems.

'And I've other things in my head, do you see? My husband has been off work with a bad chest and my eldest grandson has been dodging off school and we wants him to better himself.'

'So Matilda might have mentioned going to Pinner that day, but you don't know?' She nodded her head miserably.

'No need to blame yourself.' He patted her hand. 'You're not her mother, are you? You've got your own family to look after.' He paused. 'And I bet you one thing,' he added with a vehemence that surprised them both, 'I bet *she* didn't know what *you* were doing that evening.' His own guilt, he supposed.

There was a short, painful silence which he broke by saying in a brighter tone, 'Tell me about Matilda.'

The motherly little cook-cum-housekeeper looked perplexed.

'Helen has told me a lot, of course,' he assured her, 'but different people remember different things and see things in different ways. You might have noticed something Helen did not, particularly after she went away.'

She still looked doubtful. 'They are both very nice girls and have been very good to me.'

'I'm not asking you to be disloyal,' he protested. 'Look, let me tell you what I know.' He ticked off on his fingers one by one. 'She was young, pretty – and rather shy – but had gained confidence since she had taken up selling the paintings . . . '

'She used to cry when she first had to do that,' said Mrs Briggs, suddenly angry. 'Poor thing.' Her eyes shot guiltily towards the door. 'But, of course, when Helen explained to her why she had to do it . . . '

'Helen has the stronger personality?'

'Oh, yes,' she nodded, and smiled fondly, 'like her father.'

'Does Matilda mind?'

'Well she *is* very under Helen's thumb. But she is very proud of her clever sister and thinks most of the things she does are right.'

'But not all of them?'

'Well, no. She is more, I don't know ... more like a proper girl. More ladylike and demure.' She took a deep breath and with another brief glance towards the door said quickly, 'Helen does think some funny things, you know.'

He did.

'Nothing wicked, of course, just, just ...'

'Advanced? Different?'

She seemed happy with those words, accepting them gratefully. 'Yes, that's it, advanced and – different. She's so clever, you see.'

'But Matilda is the pretty one.'

'Oh yes, she's beautiful.' Her eyes lit up at the thought. 'So fair, and delicate.'

'How does Helen feel about having such a pretty sister?'

She looked puzzled at the question, 'Oh, she likes it, of course. And it comes in handy, doesn't it? Selling the paintings.' Mrs Briggs paused, then said, 'But she's not jealous of her or anything if that's what you're meaning. There's a big age difference you know, so they were never young girls together. When Helen was eighteen, Matilda was only seven – and Helen has had plenty of chances. She is nice-looking as well, I think,' she added protectively. 'She just takes more knowing.'

The woman was bright. A young Helen was never outshone by her exquisite sister. She could still resent such easy favour now, however. He wondered why he was pursuing this line but somehow felt impelled to continue. 'And they look so different. One so fair, the other so dark.'

'Oh, that's because they had different mothers! Helen's died when she was only eight.'

He was taken aback. Why hadn't she mentioned that? Maybe she didn't think it was important. It might make for some feelings though. He was on to something, he just felt it.

'Do they quarrel much?'

'Oh no!' Mrs Briggs thought for a moment, absently brushing escaping stray hairs back towards her bun. 'Honestly, I can't say they do that. 'Course, they do have a dust-up now and then. Everybody does, don't they?'

They do, he agreed. Even he and his lovely Emma used to have a few angry words now and then. He would take every one of them back if only he could hold her again.

'It was just that some of the things they did, I mean do, make Matilda feel uncomfortable, but she doesn't like to say anything because she knows how hard her sister works to keep them and, anyway, she thinks Helen knows best.'

'So you can't see Matilda running away, leaving home – to get away from her sister?'

'No! Oh no. After their father died they clung to each other.'

Best nodded sympathetically. 'Very hard that they were left with very little money.'

She looked a bit nonplussed, 'Yes . . .'

'Weren't they?' he asked very casually.

'Well . . . well, I don't know that much about how they are set up, of course,' she said offering the requisite servant's denial of in-depth knowledge, 'but of course there was Matilda's inheritance from her Aunt Augusta.'

'Oh?' As Best's senses quivered acutely, his most offhand manner switched on automatically. He shrugged. 'But I expect that didn't amount to much?'

'Oh yes it did,' she assured him. 'It came to a lot – I think. They were very excited about it at the time anyways. 'Course, they was a bit disappointed that they couldn't get much of it straight away.'

'What a shame. Why was that?'

'Well, someone, I don't know who, was – what they said? – "holding it" for Matilda until she came of age.' She began to look about nervously again. 'But Miss Helen will tell you all that.'

Oh she will, will she, thought Best? She hasn't so far. 'Oh, I remember – she did mention something,' he lied. 'Must have slipped my mind – that's why it helps to talk to someone else – reminds me of things I missed.' He smiled and tapped his head to indicate his own inadequacy.

'I suppose the amount she got straight away went on clearing up their father's debts?'

Mrs Briggs looked nonplussed, then nodded vaguely. 'I suppose so. That and Helen's trip to Paris, of course.'

'Oh, of course, of course,' he nodded, as though that, too, had slipped his foolish mind.

'An investment, Miss Helen called it.'

'I expect Matilda would have rather spent it on pretty clothes!' laughed Best.

'I'm sure,' Mrs Briggs nodded fondly.

'So, should anything happen to Matilda' – he stopped short when he saw how this suggestion affected the cook-housekeeper – 'which I'm sure it won't, of course,' he added hastily, 'the money would all go to Helen?'

'There isn't anyone else, is there?'

Best didn't know. He didn't know anything any more. For some reason he felt a weary disappointment at the heart of him. He reminded himself that he really didn't like Helen Franks. But he had somehow trusted her. Accepted her story unequivocally. Thought her honourable. And that didn't happen often. What he did know, he thought, bringing himself back to the job in hand, was that Mrs Briggs was clearly a witness to cultivate – but slowly. He could see that when he paused she was already becoming nervous that she had said too much and was troubled by the implication of his final question. Better get back to safer ground.

'Now,' he said quietly, proffering a list written on blue paper in his neat but slightly florid hand, 'I want you to look at this and tell me if you can think of anything else of Matilda's that is missing. Take your time.'

It contained a change of underwear, spare gloves and handkerchiefs, a nightdress and a few trinkets. All indicating that Matilda certainly intended to stay away, but possibly only for a night. Mrs Briggs took it but didn't look at it.

'You can read?' he asked gingerly.

'Of course!' She was indignant. 'I went to St Saviour's Church School until I was ten and I was always one of the best readers in Miss O'Connor's class! No,' – she put the list down on the table – 'it's just that yesterday I noticed something else that was gone.' She twisted her damp hankie in her lap. 'It gave me a turn when I realized and' – the emotion began to choke her – 'made me think she might have meant to stay away for ever!'

Best touched her hand and said softly, 'And what was that, Mrs Briggs?'

'Her raggedy doll!'

'It was important to her?'

'She would never be parted from it. Her mother made it for her from scraps from her workbasket. It was a poor wee thing, that doll, been patched and mended, patched and mended . . . '

'She would take it to Pinner with her?'

Mrs Briggs shook her head, 'No. But she would have taken it if she never meant to come back!'

After a decent interval spent slowly taking details of Matilda's raggedy doll Best got back to business. 'Had you noticed anything different about Matilda lately?'

'Different?'

'Was she happier? Sadder?'

'Oh, she was always a cheerful girl,' Mrs Briggs exclaimed, pushing the wristbands of her blouse back briskly as though about to roll out some pastry. 'But now you come to mention it, she did seem even happier than usual.' As she spoke Helen re-entered the room. 'Full of life, glowing really and always singing to herself. Didn't even seem to mind going off to sell the paintings, or to one of them artists' houses to model.'

Best was stunned. 'Say that again!'

'F-full of life er . . . '

'No! The last bit.' Fury was now growing in him. 'The very last bit!' He turned to glare at the suddenly rigid Helen.

'To . . . to model,' whispered a startled Mrs Briggs. 'That's what she said . . . ' She looked nervously back and forth from the furious Best to the blushing Helen.

'I don't believe it!' he exclaimed. 'I just don't believe it!'

'Oh dear what have I–'

'You have done nothing, Mrs Briggs. It's your mistress who has been less than honest with me! Criminally so!' He turned to glare at her again. 'You amaze me, Miss Franks! You really do!'

Mrs Briggs had gone, leaving Best and Helen Franks facing each other stonily across the plush-covered surface of the parlour table. She, looking neat and contained in a snugly fitting navy dress with a lace trim at the neck and wrists, making Best suddenly aware of the delicacy of her fair skin. He remained very angry, particularly as his outburst against her had failed to elicit any apology or excuse for withholding vital evidence beyond a stiff statement that she had her reasons and that they were good ones. Also, that she was convinced that Matilda's occasional artistic posing had nothing whatsoever to do with her disappearance and that, in any case, she had made her own enquiries in that direction which had confirmed this opinion.

'Why,' said Best acidly, 'did you bother to do *that* if you were already convinced enquiries would be of no avail?'

She refused to respond to this comment keeping the gaze of her hazel eyes fixed on a silver-framed picture in her hand as he spoke. He wanted to slap that pink and white cheek very hard.

'I'll tell you this, Miss Franks, unless you co-operate with me and give me full details of all Matilda's contacts, I will withdraw from this enquiry. My superiors will support me and see that no other officer is required to waste his time as I feel I have.'

She looked up sharply. 'You can't withdraw from a murder enquiry! I must know whether she is dead or alive!'

'I will not withdraw from the murder enquiry. But we have no proof whatsoever that your sister is the victim. As far as we are concerned she is merely a missing person – an adult missing person – whom we have no obligation to trace. She is perfectly entitled to leave home, leave the country, leave this planet, should she wish, without any interference from us.' What was it about her that enraged him so?

'She was seen walking near the scene!'

'That proves nothing! If you are convinced that your sister may be the canal explosion victim and want us to pursue that possibility, I demand your full co-operation and any knowledge of anything which may back up that possibility.'

Helen contemplated the orange flowers decorating the green tablecloth absently tracing the outline of one of the larger blooms with her left index finger while in her other hand she still grasped the silver frame. Suddenly she looked small, defeated and weary but Best remained firm. He'd been fooled by her before, he reminded himself.

'Very well,' she murmured softly.

'What?' he snapped. 'I didn't hear you.'

She looked up and straight at him, sighed and more loudly did her penance. 'Very well, I said,' she paused, then rallied again. 'But you knew that, didn't you?'

'I had to be sure,' he rejoined, allowing only a small smile of triumph to light his lips.

The light was fading fast. Best gazed out of the full-length windows at the crowd of merrymakers strolling around the Eyre Arms Pleasure Gardens, the ladies' gowns glowing like butterfly wings against the dark suits of their partners. Garlands of ornamental lanterns began springing into life, their beams causing jewels to wink and glitter like fireflies. He was transfixed. Best took a childlike delight in all things bright and beautiful. A legacy from his Italian mother, he felt, although she would not own it, claiming Italians had more taste. According to her, he had acquired his love of the gaudy from his English father. Others saw that it was his vivacity he should attribute to her.

With some effort, he dragged his attention back to the serious business about to take place around the long oak table – the inaugural meeting of the Regent's Canal Explosion Relief Committee. Even this worthy gathering also had its more colourful side he noticed. Two or three 'artistic gentlemen' with floppy cravats and exotic embroidered waistcoats made the Sergeant's attire appear positively discreet. He recognized them as successful artists who had no need to excuse their flamboyance, indeed, it was expected of them. The rest were sober-suited businessmen straight from the City, and a sprinkling of worthy clerics.

Many of those assembled had houses in the explosion area and so could class themselves as victims, but their stated agenda that evening was to find ways of assisting the poorer victims of the blast. That, and to consider the remedies of all – at law. They deemed it their first duty, 'before hearts grow cold', to make the decision to apply to the Lord Mayor to set up a public subscription.

As Best had expected, it did not take long for the matter of members' insurance claims to take centre stage. Suddenly, one man, an MP, proclaimed piously, 'I will be no party to any of the funds collected being used for the purpose of litigation.'

Since no one had suggested any such thing, there was some tightening of lips at this cynical seizing of moral ascendancy particularly when members of the Press were present. There was also a great deal of head nodding and calls of 'Hear, Hear!' Nodding particularly vigorously, the Sergeant noted, was the domed, pink head of Mr Van Ellen and that of a young man beside him whose features were of a similar cherubic appearance. The look sat better on the younger man. Who was he? Most likely another son. Odd that Van Ellen hadn't mentioned another son. But then, had they asked? *Should I be doing another job*, Best chastised himself? *I certainly seemed to be failing at this one.*

'There has been much talk of dangers on the canal, but what about the tumbril after tumbril of gunpowder which passes up Oxford Street daily?' asked a Mr Pratt, to loud applause.

'At least the railways are safe! We ought to be grateful to them for that!' exclaimed Mr Van Ellen.

But when someone else tried, long-windedly, to take up this safety angle he was brought back to the main aim by one of the clergymen who pointed out that, 'The cold wind blowing between the rough boards which still form the windows of the houses of the poor make the need for relief urgent.'

Another cleric pointed out that small shopkeepers had also been hard hit. Shop-fronts were damaged and windows broken. Then there were the lodging-house keepers who had lost residents as a result of rooms made uninhabitable by damage from falling plaster and glass. Not only that, lodgers were fearful of returning to the houses in case they fell down or there was another explosion.

Having seized the floor, the reverend gentleman held on to it.

'Schoolmistresses, too, are having to turn away their pupils,' he continued, passionately, 'and, worst of all, laundresses have had their finished washing dirtied again by falling plaster and now, not only have to wash it all again without extra payment, but also have to buy more coal and coke at one shilling and eight pence a sack with which to do it. Such a loss is not a small one to such poor and hard-working people,' he ended, looking accusingly around his dazed audience who, plainly, had never had to consider life in terms of re-dirtied laundry and the price of coke.

The clergyman's impassioned appeal bore fruit. When the gathering dispersed soon after, the chairman's table was, as *The Times* reported later, 'agreeably covered with bank notes.'

But, before the meeting was formally closed, Best was allowed time to make an appeal for information regarding any missing young ladies and went on to field many eager questions about the progress of the police enquiries.

Then a reporter tried to provoke Best into voicing suspicions about the Fenians and added, 'And what about the war between the railways and the canals? Have you considered that?'

'War?' countered Best innocently, 'I didn't realize feelings ran that high . . . ' Out of the corner of his eye he saw Van Ellen and his companion leaving. That was an acquaintance he wouldn't have minded renewing – in the informal manner this occasion afforded.

'He'd tell you more about that,' said the reporter, following his glance.

'A shareholder?' smiled Best, careful not to betray his quickened interest.

He grinned wickedly, 'That's an understatement.'

'With the railway, not the canals, I would guess?' They both laughed. 'Is that his son?'

'Yes, one of them.'

'He in the City as well?'

'Oh no! ' the man laughed. 'But Van Ellen wishes he was.'

'What then? Army or. . . ?'

'No, no, nothing like that. He's beyond the pale to Van Ellen. He's an artist – or, at least I think, would like to be.'

Chapter Ten

'I must know whether she is alive or dead!'

Helen's cry kept coming back to him as, early next morning, Best rode underground on the Metropolitan Railway.

He tried to recall her manner as she said it. With true anguish for Matilda? Or had he glimpsed self concern? Calculation, even? After all, before she could claim any of Matilda's inheritance she would need either a body or at least proof that her sister had disappeared for good. She could be using him to that end. What better ally and witness than a police officer who had done his utmost to find Matilda? She was such a cold fish it was hard to read her.

He repeated over and over again in his head, 'I must know whether she is alive or dead!' trying to remember the correct emphasis. 'I *must* know,' she had said – he was sure of that. Or was he giving emphasis on hindsight? And the expression, 'alive or dead' – wasn't that a harsh way for a loving relative to put it? More natural, surely, to have said, 'I must know what has happened to my sister!' or 'I must know where she is!'

Why should she even imagine Matilda was dead?

Yes, why? She could have run away with a lover. Many girls did. He had to admit that when Helen had first come to him she had seemed to care – been desperate even in her pleas. Oh yes, but then she was clever, Mrs Briggs had insisted on that, 'very clever' and she had needed to convince him he must take up the case.

Why hadn't she gone to her local police? Why jump to the conclusion that the body in the canal might be Matilda's? Why hold back information from him? But, maybe, that was her way of drawing him in further. Ah, but she had produced that photograph which, as Cheadle would have put it, 'took her out of the frame'. So, he was wrong. She was seriously trying to find her sister. Wasn't she?

Smoky as it was down there, Best was usually grateful that the coming of the Metropolitan Railway meant that he could now make some direct uncomplicated journeys across London. Unlike some, he didn't feel it was unnatural to travel underground – the lack of distraction gave him more time to think. This time all he seemed to be doing was getting more and more confused but comforted himself by remembering that it was often later, when he had plonked in all the ingredients, stirred them up and left them to bubble and stew for a while that a solution suddenly appeared.

Wait a minute. Wasn't it he who had unearthed the information Helen had withheld about Matilda's modelling? Had he been led into that? Could Mrs Briggs be involved? No, surely, that nice woman . . . He began to feel dizzy from chasing his own tail and from hunger. He should at least have had a slice of bread and butter before leaving home that morning. Emma would have made him.

But surely no woman could be as cold and calculating as he was imagining? He knew they could, of course, like in that recent poisoning case. Well, what was her motive – ambition? She was ambitious. She had already spent some of her sister's money on furthering that ambition and, it seemed likely that she had even deliberately avoided marriage in pursuit of that ambition! Mrs Briggs said she had had her chances, many chances. How much more proof did he need of her strangeness?

Why hadn't she told him about their different mothers? What good reason could she have? He tried to remember Helen's exact words when he first spoke to her, 'Our mother died'. That was it. Or was it just, 'Mother died', or 'Matilda's mother died'? He had been so busy just taking down the facts he had not bothered to note the form in which they had come. Of course, if she was innocent she may have thought that mentioning two mothers might have added confusion. Indeed, she might regard the second woman as a mother.

What about the fact that she had been in Paris when Matilda had gone missing? Well, they only had her word for that, hadn't they? In any case, even if she had, money could buy someone else to do your dirty work. But Matilda *had been seen* near the canal, walking towards the very bridge where the explosion took place. That couldn't be a coincidence!

One thing he was sure of was that at that moment he should not have been in what Londoners called 'the Drain', *en route* for Holland Park, but down at City Road Basin forming a welcoming party for Minchin who was due back that day.

The popping up of some pertinent factor from Best's mental stew occurred rather more quickly than usual on this occasion. Just as he was stepping out of Notting Hill Gate Station a thought hit him like a thunderbolt, shocking him far more than the sudden glare from a shaft of late autumn sun which caught him unawares as he emerged and caused him to shut his eyes abruptly.

Helen had lost two mothers – and now a sister. Wasn't that more than just bad luck?

'Don't look so ferocious, Sergeant,' said a low voice. Helen was at his elbow. She was dressed in a soft grey gown and matching short cloak trimmed with velvet, an ensemble which had the effect of making her look tiny, vulnerable and demure – quite the reverse of the demon she had become in his mind. She looked up at him with a slightly playful smile. 'After all, I *am* co-operating with you now.'

The soft grey matched her eyes. The contrast with his thoughts was too much. He felt angry. It was all a pose, this deliberate lack of vivacity in her appearance, this mouse-like sinking into the background. In reality she was a demon. 'You had no choice,' he snapped bluntly and unkindly, then shivered. Despite the brightness from the low, slanting sun, there was a distinct nip in the air. He should have worn his overcoat. Like her, the sun was deceitful.

They were on their way to the studio of the artist for whom Matilda had sat. According to Helen, the man for whom she performed this service was an old friend, 'very respectable', middle-aged and with a family on the premises. He was also an RA. When Best ventured to comment that, for such a modern woman, she was very anxious to claim repectability, Helen retorted angrily, 'It is not my obsession, Mr Best, but that of the world. We women have anxiety about respectability thrust upon us whether we like it or not!'

'But since you profess no wish to get married . . . '

'We were not discussing me! We were discussing my sister. Artists' models are given a bad reputation, no matter how innocent the circumstances. This damages their chances of marriage – or at least the choice of whom they marry.' She glared at him. 'I want Matilda to be happy.'

'I'm sure you do.' Allowing Matilda to spend her inheritance on pretty clothes instead of subsidizing a trip to Paris might also have made her happy while increasing her chances of matrimony.

As if she read his thoughts, Helen announced, 'Matilda does not need decking out like a Christmas tree to attract a husband, she is pretty enough and loveable enough without that. But she does need a good reputation – as do I so as to continue selling my works in "respectable" places. Men have no conception of the tyranny that respectability exercises over we women – and I don't think they care much either. It is to their advantage after all.'

Best said nothing. Despite appearances, she was clearly in fighting form this morning and he did not feel inclined to do battle with her. But the ensuing silence soon got the better of him and he couldn't help asking, 'But as to your reputation, would not marriage – your marriage I mean, be a help?'

'Oh yes,' she laughed bitterly, 'marriage would help me move in "respectable" circles' – the word hissed out of her – 'while denying me the time to paint. A wife's duty, don't forget, is to look after her husband and children. Would you care to hear the list of talented women artists who have fallen at that hurdle?'

Best shook his head. 'But, surely, if the man is wealthy?'

'Then I become a hostess with a charming little pastime to while away the hours while my husband is at his club. A husband who, I assure you, would not countenance his wife putting her reputation at risk by drawing from life.' She sounded as though she spoke from bitter experience, not speculation. 'In any case, I have no wish to become a rich man's plaything.' Best nearly exploded with laughter at the unlikely thought. 'I wish to remain independent.'

'I'm sure you will remain so without the least trouble!' Best retorted. Helen Franks was, he decided, the coldest and most unappealing woman he had ever set eyes on – and probably even a murderess to boot.

To his surprise she laughed out loud at his remark. 'Clearly, Sergeant, the very idea of a woman wanting to live without a man is one which you find both fascinating and incomprehensible. But I assure you I am not the only woman artist to have made this decision.' She gave him a wry, direct look. 'If it is of any comfort to you this is no reflection on the desirability of your sex.'

He felt a blush creeping up his cheeks. She had this way of making him feel foolish. Damn the woman's impertinence.

She stopped. 'Here it is.'

Judging by the imposing exterior of the double-bow-fronted, icing-sugar mansion, Jacques Bertrand was clearly one of the current darlings of the painting world. Helen Franks would be surprised to know, thought Best, that he had seen some of the artist's work at a Royal Academy exhibition when he sneaked a few minutes to look round while investigating some petty pilfering at the gallery.

A painter of ingratiating portraits of the rich and famous, and dramatic, historical tableaux, Bertrand also occasionally attempted something more daring and realistic. His *Repentance* had caused something of a sensation depicting, to some, a too earthy-seeming Christ ('might be my butcher or baker!' exclaimed one critic) bathing the feet of an over seductive-looking Mary Magdalene.

Best thought Mary was meant to be enticing, and to portray her otherwise would have been foolish. But he was well aware that was probably because policemen saw life as it really was, and not as it was pretended to be. Despite this controversy, Bertrand obviously thrived and remained the darling of his wealthy patrons.

Best had been secretly excited by the prospect of seeing a famous artist's studio and he was not disappointed. All was Eastern-style opulence. There was a musky scent in the air, rich damask covered the armchairs, colourful drapes were thrown over couches, copper pots and urns glinted and glowed in the light from the wall of windows opposite. Best had never seen a room with so much light. Decorative tall screens, so much the fashion, were used not to divide up the room into cosy corners, but described arcs from the wall where, Best presumed, they served as dressing-rooms. One was embellished with raised patterns of black and gold Chinoiserie, the other a much more homely, papier-mâché affair of flowers and birds, probably put together by someone in the Bertrand family. Emma had been working on a screen like that just before she died, only hers was a riot of mother and baby pictures cut from the pages of ladies' magazines. She had so wanted children. Doctors had warned her that to become pregnant would only hasten her inevitable end. And so it had. But she had so enjoyed creating her screen. To Best's surprise, the memory was a warm and happy one.

On a park bench on a polished wooden podium sat a young woman, dressed in rags, leaning sorrowfully over a babe in arms. Standing before an easel opposite her was a dark-haired man with a Vandyke beard, wearing loose clothes and looking, Best decided, like nothing so much as an Arab sheikh.

Seeing them, the man put his brush down and came towards Helen with outstretched arms. 'Helen, my dear,' he said warmly. His French accent was soft and slight, 'How do you bear up?' To Best's surprise, Helen returned his affectionate hug and, patting his arm, gave him a rueful look.

'We will find her, my dear, we will find her.' He spread his hands expansively, 'How can I lose my best model? It is not possible. I will not allow it.' He turned again towards Best. 'This is the young man who is to help you?'

She nodded, 'Sergeant Best of Scotland Yard. I warn you,' she continued, 'he thinks I am a difficult woman.'

'Of course you are, my dear. Of course you are,' he laughed. 'But I am sure he will do his *best* for us, will you not, Sergeant?'

Best pasted on the smile he kept specially for that little joke and tried to reciprocate in the same warm spirit but his, 'I will indeed, sir,' came out stiff and cold.

'She is not easy, I know. But she is a kind lady, this 'elen, as my wife has cause to know – and she is talented, so talented. The English, they do not appreciate talent.'

Noting Best's fascination with the set-piece he touched his arm, nodded towards his model and smiled, '*The Sick Child* – it pays the rent.' He signalled to the model to take a break before leading them over to velvet-covered chairs placed around a lacquered Chinese table. 'My clients demand civilized comfort,' he explained. 'Myself – I would be happy to paint in a bare attic.'

'What nonsense,' laughed Helen suddenly, 'you would hate it! You love all this!' Bertrand joined in her laughter then politely turned his dark, glossy eyes on Best and enquired as to how he could help.

Suddenly, Best was unsure how to proceed. Bertrand seemed to have jumped a stage in their acquaintance and was now treating him as though he was an established friend while, at the same time, he and Helen presented such an impregnable alliance he felt excluded.

Helen jumped to her feet. 'I'm sure you would both manage better if I were not here – and I want to see Marie.'

After she had left the room, Best explained that he merely wanted to discover what contacts Matilda might have made at the studio and generally fill out his picture of the girl.

Bertrand nodded and confided in that curiously intimate manner of his, 'Well, as for contacts, Officer, there is only me, my wife and my children – and the servants, of course.' He stroked his soft beard. 'They come in and out of here all of the time, you understand.' Best wondered whether that were strictly true or merely said to stress respectability.

'Your children are young?'

'Oh, yes. Five, seven, nine, eleven and fourteen.'

Best nodded, 'And the servants – are any of them male?'

The artist shook his head. 'No; oh, only except for the groom. But he is quite old – that is, if it is romance you are thinking of.'

Best shrugged. 'Possibly . . . how old?'

'About sixty-five – and not, I would imagine of any attraction to a young girl.'

'Did they have any contact?'

'Oh yes. He took her home sometimes. But I can't imagine . . . ' He shrugged.

'I'd like to see him.'

Bertrand looked surprised, 'Surely you cannot think I mean . . . old Jenkins.'

'I don't *think* anything, Mr Bertrand,' said Best, tiredly. 'He may have noticed something. He may have formed a passion for this attractive young girl. She may have confided in him as a fatherly figure now that her father is dead. Or the whole exercise might be fruitless, who knows?'

'Of course, of course. I do not think like a policeman.'

'In fact, I would like to speak to all the servants.'

Bertrand nodded understandingly. 'Ah, yes, it is they who know what is happening in any household! We are blind.' He jumped up. 'Before we talk further it is possible you would like to see some pictures of Matilda?'

'That would be very helpful.' The artist was friendly and warm but there was something about him that made Best uneasy. Was it his silkiness? Yes, that was it. He moved gracefully, his eyes and hair were glossy. He was sleek and sensuous and his manner intimate. It made Best uncomfortable. But that was no reason to distrust the man. He smiled to himself – just because he did not behave like an Englishman. Another thing, Bertrand kept touching him. He was now, as he guided him towards an ante-room. Best was not used to that any more.

From floor to ceiling the small, oblong ante-room was lined with pictures. More were stacked up on end against the far wall. Bertrand headed for the higgledy-piggledy stack and began pulling out those in which Matilda appeared: as a repentant servant girl, a devoted daughter, a young girl at her first dance, a Nordic princess and a captive of ancient Rome. Surely, Helen was jealous of such beauty? It would be only human. In all the pictures no more than a bare shoulder was displayed, such as one could see at any grand ball. Nothing to outrage anyone's susceptibilities. He must get Maitland to look at them to see whether they resembled the girl by the canal.

'Some tea is in order, I think, Sergeant?' Bertrand touched his arm and began ushering Best back into the studio.

'Oh, yes, thank you,' said Best compliantly, but resisted the apparent haste and looked about him very slowly. Most of the paintings on the wall were merely modern portraits, some half-finished.

'I put them up so when I glance at them in passing maybe I see something that is not right,' offered Bertrand. He followed Best's eyes which had just alighted on a lush Roman set-piece. 'Oh, yes, but here is one I forgot. As you see, it is not completed.'

'This is Matilda?' Best pointed to one of several toga'd Roman maidens reclining against a marble garden bench in the style of Frederick Leighton or Alma-Tadema. Roses trailed over the back of the bench catching in the girls' hair and showing up vividly against the white skin. It amused Best that the Roman maidens were all Titian or blonde while the only male figure, clearly a captive slave, was dark and sultry-looking. In reality, it would probably have been the opposite. His mother was a Roman.

'She would get to know the other sitters, of course.'

Bertrand shook his head. 'No.' He caught Best's surprise. 'Well, let us say, it is not very likely.' He amended it yet again. 'Not necessarily. You see, I work on each figure separately, so they come at different times and I tend to have a gap between them so that I may have a rest. Or,' he added, 'very often I have the one model for a whole day.'

'But when you have more than one in a day,' persisted Best, 'they may meet when they are changing over?'

He shrugged. 'I suppose so – now and then. It is possible.'

'And that would apply to the young man' – he indicated the slave figure – 'as well as the young ladies?'

Bertrand clearly did not like the way the questioning was going but nodded, 'It is possible.'

'You wouldn't remember if they did? Or in what order you did these figures?'

At this, Bertrand executed the full Gallic shrug and flung his arms wide to encompass all the pictures. 'As you see,' he pouted, '. . . it is not possible.'

Helen had just come in behind them and she said, 'If I remember correctly, Jacques, in this one you finished the female figures first, then decided that that space needed filling, and you also needed a point of tension, so you brought the young man in.'

'You are right!' Bertrand chucked his hands straight up in the air in delight. 'Of course. That is how it was, my clever *petit chou*. Didn't I tell you she was clever, Sergeant?'

'Very clever,' Best conceded without enthusiasm. He was getting sick of all this – it is possible, it is not possible. 'Nonetheless,' he added coldly, 'I will need his name and address and those of all your other sitters.'

Bertrand glanced at Helen. 'I do not think . . .'

'As I have said before, unless I have your full co-operation and that of your friends, Miss Franks, I will not proceed with this case.'

'Do tell him, Jacques.' She threw Bertrand what could only be termed a pleading glance and he appeared distinctly nervous. 'There is no harm and the Sergeant is very discreet.'

What was going on? Suddenly it came to him: these two were lovers. All these surreptitious glances, the 'old friends' intimacy. That was the reason she did not wish to marry. They were lovers – and, if he was not mistaken, they had something else to hide as well.

Chapter Eleven

Chief Inspector Arthur Amos Cheadle sat bolt upright in his chair, his huge frame motionless, his eyes glaring. He was furious again. Furious because Best had not been down at the City Road Dock that morning when Minchin's boat returned, more furious because Minchin had not been on board anyway and that the traffic manager of the Grand Junction Canal Company had had to bring this news to him. It put him at a disadvantage which he didn't like. It also made him wonder what the hell his underlings were doing.

Opposite Cheadle sat the object of his fury – a weary-looking, Sergeant Ernest Best. Next to Best, looking brighter and, like Cheadle, keeping very still but for a different reason, sat the fair and innocent-looking, PC John George Smith.

'Feel more at home with those artists, d'you?' It was more of a statement than a question.

'It was another strand of the enquiry, sir,' ventured Best.

'A strand was it, a strand!' Cheadle was derisory. 'It might be, my boy, but not a bloody urgent one! If you can't sort out which is and which ain't it's time you were back pounding the beat.'

Best said nothing. At that moment the option seemed a very good one to Best. He was sick of the Detective Branch with its overwork, long hours, loneliness. Not to mention the shelling out of money on transport and the like, and the anxiety as to whether the commissioner was going to deem it well spent and deign to refund it. Most of all he was sick of the seemingly endless complications and confusions of this case. Admittedly, walking the beat had, in the end, become boring, and the wearing of uniform both on and off duty had been very tiresome. one could never fade into the background. But right now the peace of strolling along at a measured pace without any worries seemed very attractive. It didn't help that he knew that Cheadle was right. He himself wasn't sure why he had done what he had done.

Cheadle turned his attention to the other two figures sitting to the left of his desk: Traffic Manager Albert Thornley, still worried-looking but clearly relieved to have been able to demonstrate his willingness to co-operate with the authorities. Alongside him, the darkly handsome and friendly dock labourer, Sam Grealey, as restless as ever, and looking ill-at-ease in his rough shirt and stained cord trousers tied up with string. Clearly, he didn't like being at a disadvantage either. Hadn't he done his duty, pointing out to Thornley that Minchin was missing, telling them what he knew about the man? Now he sat shifting about in his chair clenching and unclenching his strong fists and causing his considerable arm and shoulder muscles to tense and grow large which, had he known it, made him look even more out of place.

'Near Tring, you said?'

Thornley nodded. 'Coming into Marsworth – "Maffers" the boatmen call it – there's a run of seven locks there. He got out to see the boat through, then went off. The crew thought he'd gone to pass water, but he never came back.'

'Been drinking? Fell in the canal?'

'Drink's forbidden on our boats.'

The Chief Inspector didn't even bother to comment, merely let a slight sardonic smile twitch his lips as Thornley continued.

'Look, I know boatmen have a reputation, but not only is it exaggerated, they're kept at it on these fly runs, don't get much of a chance. And they know they'll lose their jobs and they're good jobs for canal folk. Anyway,' – he drew a deep breath – 'the crew swear not. They say Minchin wasn't a drinker.'

'I'm sure they do,' agreed Cheadle in the manner of one well schooled in the ways of the world. 'We will just have to ask them again, won't we?'

Thornley nodded and offered, 'In any case, be difficult to fall in accidentally there and not be seen, it's busy all the time.'

'So, he probably just scarpered?'

'Yes.'

'He have any family around there?'

'Don't know.'

'We will ask his wife.'

'Yes, sir,' said Best, 'I was going to talk to her anyway if Minchin did not come back.'

'Oh, is that right? You were going to? Well, I don't want you to do that now.'

'Sir?'

'That's a job for Constable Smith.' He put on a mock posh voice, 'You, Sergeant Best, will proceed in a northerly direction – to Berkhamsted – in pursuit of Mr Minchin. You remember that quaint old police habit, pursuit?'

'Yes, sir.'

Cheadle could scarcely contain his pleasure. 'And you will go by canal.'

It was Best's turn to sit bolt upright. 'Sir?' He hesitated. 'But surely, the train is much faster?'

'Well, well, suddenly Sergeant Best is in a hurry to find Mr Minchin.' The Chief Inspector had relaxed enough to allow himself to begin his usual slow descent down in his chair. 'Might be faster, Sergeant, but not by that much because you will be leaving tonight on one of the fly boats. Then you can get to know canals, canal boats and canal people on your journey and you can gather clues – you remember them? – so no time will be wasted. Fill out the picture for you, won't it?'

'Yes, sir.' Best was horrified. Those dirty little boats!

'You've seen to that?' Cheadle asked Thornley.

'Yes. We've taken a bit of cargo off the *Yarmouth* to make space.'

'He won't need much,' said Cheadle, with a grin. The image of the immaculate Best cramped in a filthy boat among bags of coal clearly delighted him. One day, thought Best, I will hit him.

Constable Smith saw no signs of bruising on Mrs Minchin's face and arms – something Best had told him to look out for. Standing before him on the doorstep of number seven, Alma Street, a lodging-house close by the City Road Basin, he saw just a typical, working-class woman such as he saw every day on his beat. Cleaner than many, she was thin and pale, with a babe-in-arms and a rather unappealing, bare-footed toddler clinging to her skirts. Probably in her early thirties but looking almost ten years older. Not pretty, and probably never had been, but with a certain air about her, a dignity, as though she had been meant for better things. That, and a pervading sadness.

The sight of him, still so obviously an official of some sort despite Best's ministrations, had agitated her. She had stared at him and grasped her baby tighter.

'Is it . . . Joe?' she asked. 'What's happened to him. . . ? Tell me!'

That answered one question for Smith straight away. No, four in fact. She was waiting for him to come back, didn't know where he was, cared that he hadn't returned and his not coming home was unusual.

When the fair-haired young man confessed that he had no idea where Joe was, she relaxed a little. No news was better than bad news. Of course, this concern of hers might be because her husband was the breadwinner. If he didn't come back they might starve.

He invited himself in in the friendly manner with which he had seen Best gain entry. The small boy in the background who had been staring at Smith thundered along the wooden corridor ahead of them to open the door of their room. Smith winked at him and he grinned and came and sat beside him. Now for the difficult part.

Mrs Minchin was obviously expecting to hear more from him about where Joe might be. He wanted the same from her, but without sounding the alarm or upsetting her unduly. He mustn't even hint that Joe might be an adulterer and even a murderer. For the same reasons he decided not to tell her he was a policeman. She seemed to assume he was a company official and he left it at that.

'Can you think where Joe might be?'

'No. Didn't you ask his mates? I was only told he didn't get back on the boat after he was at some locks.'

'That's right. That's right. He's not stayed away before, then?'

'No. He always comes back when he says. Never stayed away before, 'cept when they didn't get the loading done in time.' She plucked nervously at her baby's vest. She might not be bruised physically – where you could see anyway – but she seemed injured somehow.

'No relatives or friends up Tring way?'

'No, we comes from Bethnal Green. 'Course, he might have met someone on the boats. But he don't make friends easy.'

She didn't seem to know anything, or, at least, said she didn't, but she might be lying. Until he had become a policeman he had never realized how much people lied to officials and it had shocked him when he found out.

'He's got no relatives he goes to see, then? His mum or ... '

'Oh yes. He goes to see his mum. But he always says first.'

He couldn't, shouldn't ask her, but he had to. He did it like a joke. 'Not got a lady-friend nowhere, then?'

Her mouth dropped open and she looked at him aghast.

'Just my little joke, Mrs Minchin. My little joke.' He forced a chuckle.

She clearly thought his little joke not very funny and was near to tears. Smith rushed on, 'I expect he just accidentally missed the boat. Maybe he was tired and had a little nap. It's a hard job. He's a good workman and I'm sure the company wouldn't want to lose him.'

She nodded. 'He only went 'cos we needed the extra money.'

He was at a loss at how to continue and he felt she was looking at him strangely as though wondering why the company had sent such a clumsy young man to see her. Best would know what to say next. He was a past master at keeping things going and finding things out from people without them realizing they were giving things away.

Mrs Minchin was struggling to say something. 'His pay – we was waiting for his pay ... ' She blushed as though it were not right to be asking.

'I'll speak to the manager, Mrs Minchin, don't you worry. Meanwhile' – he reached in his pocket and gave her a shilling – 'this will help you get a meal today.'

Relieved, she took pity on the awkward young man and offered him a cup of tea. He accepted gratefully, time to think what else he could ask and maybe look around.

Best's mother was taking him to Italy, as she had always promised to do, but they were on a train and he couldn't get her to understand that trains did not travel on water. They would have to alight and get on the boat for that section of the journey. The train driver seemed to be in her thrall for he attempted the journey nonetheless. Best rushed around, trying to find his mother who had stalked off when he argued with her, and, at the same time, trying to prevent the inevitable tragedy. But the water had come pouring in and the train, bumping and heaving, began to slide, hissing and groaning, under the waves.

He had begun to scream out in terror when a particularly heavy thump awakened him. His immediate relief was cut short by the fact that he could not work out where he was. It was dark, there was bumping and grinding outside and he could hear water sloshing about. He struck out and found himself in a wooden box. Oh God! He *was* in a sinking train! Suddenly, a heavy hessian curtain was dragged back and, in the welcoming light, a weather-worn hand appeared bearing a tin mug of steaming-hot tea. The captain was looking down on him. Best wondered if he looked as terrified as he felt.

He had boarded the boat at Paddington Basin and straight away been shown his bunk, a straw pallet on an iron-hard board in the corner of a stuffy cabin, but he had been so exhausted that no sooner had he lay down than he had fallen into a deep sleep. The first fifteen miles they just glided silently along but eventually they came to a lock with all the shouting, the bumping and grinding of the boat against the lock-sides and the hiss of the water as it poured in to raise them to the next level, but on he slept, the sounds and movement weaving themselves into his dream.

The scalding tea was strangely flavoured, very weak, very sweet, and milkless. Nonetheless, it restored Best to some degree of normality. More was achieved when, to his surprise, the boat's lad appeared, handed him a nobbly scrap of rough yellow soap and a small, coarse towel and indicated a bowl of hot water for his morning wash.

While he cleaned himself up, two of the crew settled themselves into the bunk he had just vacated, the lad took over the steering and the captain began to get busy with a frying pan. Best got out of their way and perched himself on the wooden plank on top of the load, dangling his legs over the tarpaulin.

Leaving behind a small, rural lock lined with pretty cottages, their gardens dotted with yellow, gold and white chrysanthemums, they reached a stretch as wide as a river. Off to the right, the dark-lined furrows of a newly ploughed field; in the woods to the left, glimmers of early morning sun touched the gold and flame-red leaves.

All was peaceful, bar the chirruping and twittering of the birds who had been up for hours. Intermingled now with sweet musty smells of autumn was the heavenly aroma of frying bacon as the captain busied himself over the small stove. Best was famished. Already breakfasting, a family of rabbits munched steadily at the dew-moist grass, and a kingfisher flashed by, dipping towards the water and away again with a small fish glinting in its beak. Best, the city boy, was enchanted. Despite the chill in the air and his stiffness from sleeping in such cramped conditions, he began to smile.

Mrs Minchin was in the communal kitchen making tea. Meanwhile, Smith, under the unrelenting gaze of the small boy, wandered around the sparsely furnished room, attempting to appear merely thoughtful as he strove to find some clue as to where Minchin might be – a letter on the mantelpiece, a bus or pawn ticket. There was nothing. In fact, the only sign of the written word was on the side of a dented tin, long since empty of its Bennetts Assorted Biscuits.

Suddenly the lad was peering up at him earnestly. 'You know where my dad is?' He must have been about five or six years old. Maybe more, but undersized.

'No, son. But don't worry, I expect he'll be back soon.'

The boy did not seem specially cheered by this thought. He hitched up his right sock and enquired abruptly, 'You got a pencil? I 'ad one but it's gawn.'

'Yes, son. In fact, I've got two pencils. What's your name?'

'George.'

'Well, George,' – he fished in his jacket pocket – 'I have a big one and a little one.'

He brought out the short stub he had been using up and handed it to the lad who snatched it, then grinned. 'Fanks.'

On the mangled remnants of a brown paper-bag George soon demonstrated his ability not only to draw cats, dogs and houses but to name them – after a fashion. He made no attempt, however, to depict Mum, or Dad, or Grandma.

'What about your . . .' Smith began, but hesitated as George began to scrawl laboriously under a drawing of a three-storey house. Two wobbly words later he looked up expectantly. 'M A R – what does that say?' Smith asked. 'Mar – Martha?'

Little George nodded vigorously and looked pleased.

'Now, that second word. . . ?' Under the eager gaze of the boy, Smith struggled until he began to realize that the second word began with a capital E which had gone terribly wrong and was followed by a 'u' – or was it a 'v'? Clearly the next letter was an 'a', there was no doubt about that.

'It's Hevans, Marfa Hevans, 'course,' George announced finally, unable to wait any longer for his slow-witted friend. His tone suggested that everyone knew who she was.

'Who's she, George?'

George was taken aback. 'You know – where my dad goes sometimes.'

'Oh, yes. 'Course. I forgot.'

He could hear the clink of cups and saucers as Mrs Minchin approached, but before she opened the door he managed to whisper, 'I've forgotten where that is, George, will you take me?'

George was delighted with this idea, 'Yeah, 'course,' he said, jumping instantly to his feet and making for the street door.

Mrs Minchin was opening the other door as Smith whispered quickly, 'No, in a minute, when we've had our tea.' He put a finger to his lips and winked. 'Just our secret, eh?' The lad nodded eagerly, put a grimy finger to his lips and struggled to wink back but managed only to screw up both eyes simultaneously.

Best ate his breakfast sitting on the edge of the little stern deck at the captain's feet. The captain was back at the tiller. It was a mercy that the deck looked reasonably clean, thought the Sergeant. It was acting as a plate for the doorstep slices of bread and butter which accompanied his egg and bacon but he was too hungry to care. He was beginning to appreciate that there were some advantages in this compact simple living. Everything to hand, few problems and possessions to worry about.

The more tiresome side of canal life reasserted itself when another run of locks loomed. The Sergeant, spirits still high as the day blossomed into one of autumn's golden best, decided that this was just the time to get out his homework and do his thinking. He walked ahead and found himself a perch on a pile of logs at the top of the run of locks, wiped off the dew with his (unusually grubby) handkerchief, and began reading.

The Fenians were out of the picture. Best was sure of that now. The more he thought about the inquest evidence the more it seemed feasible to him that the experts were right.

The explosion had been an accident and that would rule out dirty work by the railways as well. In any case, since the railways appeared to be winning the war what point would there be in them sabotaging the canals in such a cynical and lethal manner? He crossed both off his list along with the Somers Town barmaid. The Investigating Inspector had found more witnesses as to the cellarman's passion for Liza Moody as well as some of her garments among the man's meagre belongings. He had concluded that it was, as it appeared to be, a murder followed by a related suicide and, Best realized, with no likely connection to his Regent's Canal body.

He could concentrate on who she was, how she got into the canal and who put her there. So what did he have left? Not much: there was a girl not unlike the victim who had been seen walking towards the canal the evening before and who had a sister with good reason to wish her dead.

There was a so far unexplained row overheard at St Pancras Basin on the night in question as the *Tilbury* passed through, and angry words left on the wall later. Coupled with that was the vague possibility that an evangelist was involved.

There was the missing Limehouse woman in the Thames case. Sayers' latest report which he had just read gave him further details as he had requested. She had indeed been young, and fair so it had not been surprising that the the dock-labourer husband and the anxious neighbour had failed to identify the gruesome remains as being hers. She also had blue eyes and a circular scar on her right shoulder. That crossed her off Best's list. His victim had no such scar.

His pencil was poised to delete her when he thought, just a minute though. It had been the husband who had described the scar and it was clear that Sayer was not happy about him. Indeed the neighbour felt if she did have a scar he had probably put it there. If she did not have a scar, what better way to prevent her identification than to make one up? Perhaps a little bit unlikely, Best had to concede, but for now he left the girl from Limehouse on his list.

And then there was Joe Minchin, the surly man who had helped load the *Tilbury* that night. The man who had woman trouble. The man who had scratches on his face. The man who had gone missing. The murderer surely?

Mrs Minchin had shown no surprise when little George followed big John George Smith out into the street and skipped off ahead of him. It was the way of small boys, following people. Two of his friends joined him. One an older, taller boy with a wall eye and crooked teeth was sporting boots which looked almost new, unusual in these parts. The other, younger and smaller, wore shoes which were collapsing all about him although he seemed oblivious of the fact.

The little posse trotted down to the City Road where they turned left towards the City. They paused to look over a bridge into the City Road Basin before turning left again between a timber yard and a manufacturer's of patent capsules. They were in Wharf Road which ran between the two canal basins; the City Road and Wenlock. There was only one turning off to the right before Wharf Road became a long unbroken tunnel of factories and warehouses. They took it.

Smith was excited. Wait till Best heard this! He had found Minchin's sweetheart! He might even find Minchin! But the boy's skipping was becoming aimless.

'Where are we going?' Smith shouted to him.

'Dunno!' he shouted back.

'But you said you knew!'

Little George stopped suddenly and looked back, offended. 'I do, mister! I do! It's just up there . . . near . . . near school.'

Smith apologized and gave himself into the care of the confident young George. No sense in spoiling it now. On and on they went until suddenly, young George stopped and pointed eagerly at the centre of a row of shops beside the Eagle Tavern. Minchin's woman must be a shop assistant or ... PC Smith's heart sank to the woolly socks handknitted by his mother. There, alongside the familiar three golden spheres, was writ large, MARY EVANS, Jewellers and Pawnbrokers.

Smith, who was still young enough to expect life to fulfil its rosy promises, was crestfallen. The chipped and tarnished gold balls taunted him. Of course! Everyone around here used the pawnshop. Those as poor as the Minchins would probably be back and forth to the pawnshop regularly. They didn't sing about going up and down the City Road, in and out the Eagle, and popping the weasel for nothing.

He had been silly to follow a small child. George grinned up at him, pleased with himself. 'Didn't I tell you, mister?' He hitched up both his socks in celebration and awaited approval.

Smith patted his head. 'Well done, son, well done.' Suddenly, a thought occurred, 'This Mary Evans, is she pretty?'

'Nah, she's an ugly old gel,' said the older boy, obviously blissfully unaware of his own shortcomings in that department,

'You going in there to 'ave a bet mister?'

Chapter Twelve

It was a great foolishness to remove him from the scene of action for so long at such a vital time, thought Best. Trails grew colder by the minute.

The fly boats were gliding along the high ridge of the Tring Summit Level which was shared, somewhat ironically, by the tracks of the London/Birmingham railway. Soon they would begin going downhill again but before they reached Marsworth Junction, Best's destination, there would be a run of no less than seven locks to work through. He decided to walk the rest of the way.

The late afternoon was pleasant, the air was fresh and he needed the exercise. In any case, he was becoming impatient of the slow progress. The sooner he got to Marsworth the sooner he would be back where his presence mattered. Nonetheless, he would be the first to admit that the rest and change had done him good and he strode out on to the sunlit towpath with a lively step and a whistle on his lips.

The path was busy. He dodged towing horses waiting for their boats to pass through the locks and hordes of unkempt children playing while doing the same. He acknowledged greetings from boat people and fishermen on the bankside, obviously bemused to see such a spruce and dapper gent striding along their lowly towpath. Some of the children were so affected by the sight they upped and followed him, Pied Piper-like, until called back by their parents.

Below and to his left, glinting in the slanting sunlight were two of the three huge reservoirs built to hold the water necessary to keep the locks operating. Many of the water birds they gave home to were new to Best, although he did recognize the mallards, tufted ducks and crested grebes common to London's parks. The queue of colourful boats were making magical reflections in the murky waters of the canal. Even the more decrepit and dirtier kind managed to look quite appealing in their mirror image.

The news he received when he reached Marsworth brought him up sharp. A telegraph awaited him. It was from Cheadle:

Proceed immediately to Braunston – missing woman,
Mary Elizabeth Jones, answers description. Letter follows.

Well, at least he wouldn't be expected to go the rest of the way by boat. With the aid of the lock-keeper's railway guides he set to work. He could catch the train either by going north a few miles to Cheddington or south back to Tring, from where he would travel to Rugby. Trouble was, he could not get to either station in time for the next train in an hour's time and there wasn't another for four hours. Then, of course, when he arrived in Rugby it would be late and so most unlikely he would be able to obtain a horse and trap to take him to Braunston at that hour. That would mean he would have to stay overnight and incur more expense. He sighed. Not only would it be cheaper but probably quicker, and a great deal less of a headache just to stay on the canal.

Now, his boat had to complete the run down the locks to Marsworth, then up another run on the other side towards Leighton Buzzard. He decided to utilize the time by doing what he came to do in the first place, trace up Minchin.

Having come to a dead end with 'Mary Evans', PC Smith decided to begin work on Best's list of male artists' models to see if they could tell him anything the police did not already known about Matilda Franks. He didn't feel entirely dejected by the Minchin episode, consoling himself with the thought that at least he had discovered that the man was a regular gambler – which could mean something.

Giving some money to Mrs Minchin had made things a little more difficult for him. To make up for the loss he would have to walk a bit more, but he was used to that. Divisional detectives and their assistants always had to walk the first three miles before becoming eligible for travel expenses – something the Yard men didn't have to suffer.

Number one on his list proved wonderfully handsome and eager to assist, but somehow told him very little having only met Matilda twice and then only briefly. Numbers two and three were obviously effeminate and, while agreeing they had spoken to Matilda in passing, were clearly much more excited by their recollections of sharing the artistic stage with the beautiful number one. About him, they could remember a great deal. About Matilda, not much. When they began commenting on Smith's well-developed torso being very paintable, he beat a hasty retreat.

The fourth man was quite elderly, obviously used by Bertrand to portray an old beggar, a blind man, a wise old senator or a young maiden's grandfather. He had no recollection whatsoever of meeting Matilda, but Smith suspected his recent recollections on any subject were somewhat limited.

The fifth man, Montague Price, would have seemed more at home holding a straight bat on the playing fields of Eton than gracing a historical tableau in an artist's studio: fair, clean-cut, impeccably English, with a slightly supercilious manner softened by a touch of humour in his pale-blue eyes.

'Yes, of course I knew Matilda. A very pretty girl. Knew both girls, in fact.'

'Both?' Smith was puzzled.

'Yes, Matilda and Helen.'

'Helen posed as well?'

'Oh, no, no. Helen is the painter. She took lessons.'

'From Bertrand? You mean when Matilda sat?'

Price waved his hand correctively. 'Only sometimes. She was just a member of our class and sometimes we were there when Matilda was posing and sometimes not.'

Smith felt at sea. 'Your class. I don't understand. I thought you were a model?'

'I'm both, old boy. I'm a budding artist for my sins, who earns a crust with a spot of posing. Pater cut me off when I said I wanted to paint. Not an unusual story, I can assure you.'

'And Mr Bertrand gives you lessons?'

'Correct, Constable. Master classes he calls them. For myself and others, of course. A group of about ten.'

'A mixed group?'

'Well, Helen was the only lady, until she went off to Paris, now we are all male.'

Smith was stunned by this new turn. 'Male young men?'

Price laughed uproariously then said, 'Well, maybe not – you've seen some of them!'

Smith blushed and stuttered, 'I didn't mean . . . I mean, what I did mean was it's just that we didn't realize that there were other young men coming to the studio besides models. It, it . . . complicates things.' He felt foolish, but struggled to adjust his thoughts and think of the kind of questions Best would ask. Was he missing something again – like he had at the Three Tuns? His next question, when it came, came out clumsily. 'These young men, were any of them particularly friendly with Matilda?'

Price hesitated very slightly before saying casually, 'Not that I noticed, old boy. But then, I wouldn't. Too busy learning the elements, don't you know. Getting things in perspective.' He grinned. 'Hopeless at that I am, judging where the disappearing point should be ... '

Joseph Minchin had last been seen going off to relieve himself by the final locks in the approach to Marsworth. Where had he gone after that, and why? Not for the first time Best wished he knew more about the man. The main impression, gained at the inquest was of a gaunt, sullen, non-communicative man. Woman trouble, Grealey had claimed. But maybe Minchin had merely been bored with his fellow workman's chatter, or justifiably worried that the inquest might reveal some carelessness which could cost him his job. In the event, that seemed not to be the case. True, carelessness had been revealed but largely of a general kind pointing more to lack of good management. The revelation, of course, could still affect Minchin's job.

He might have been afraid of revelations about the woman victim but those, too, had not as yet transpired. But why, if he was innocent of the murder, had he gone missing? Was he trying to escape woman trouble? Did he fear the police were on his track? If so, what had given him that idea? Must have been something definite; he didn't seem like a man who would panic. And how do you know that, Best chastised himself. You saw him once, side view, for a few minutes – and heard a little about him from his colleague, Grealey, and boss, Albert Thornley – both of whom may have had their own reasons for blacking Minchin.

Maybe Minchin had stolen the woman one of them wanted? Seemed a bit unlikely. Thornley was too pre-occupied with his work to get up to that kind of thing and a well set-up man like Grealey could surely outshine

Minchin? But you could never be certain about such things. For example, he had never heard Minchin speak and people could alter before your eyes as soon as they did that. The charms of a pretty girl could diminish swiftly and, conversely, her plainer sister could flower and begin to wind herself into your dreams, and you could begin to wonder how you ever imagined she was plain! Take Helen Franks. She had seemed so colourless when he had first seen her but now seemed to make many of her brighter sisters seem flashy, silly and frivolous. But then, she was an accomplished deceiver, wasn't she? A murderess, even? He shook all thoughts of her from his mind. Or tried to.

Back to business. Why had Minchin gone missing at Marsworth of all places? Was this where the murder had taken place? Did he have some unfinished business with regard to the deed, some telltale tracks to eliminate? Did he have friends here? Or was there something else about this place? Best gazed across the canal up over the sloping fields dotted with grazing horses to the squat Norman tower of Marsworth village church. From here, it looked a quiet, peaceful, pretty little spot. What could Minchin have wanted here? He must go up into the village to investigate – if he had time.

But first, he should look again at the precise place where the missing man had last been seen – back alongside the locks which ran down into Marsworth. He stood outside the junction offices on the west side of the canal, in a triangle of land formed by the Grand Junction, which here curved off north eastwards, and the narrow Aylesbury Arm which turned west dropping down abruptly and spectacularly to the plain below. Retracing his steps he climbed over one of the Aylesbury Arm locks, and gazed down the steep staircase of seven locks, on to the picturesque bridge and white house which sat at the bottom of the drop, and then over to Aylesbury in the distance. A delightful scene, unbelievably pretty. This was better than following criminals up the dingy Caledonian Road! Had Minchin been similarly struck and decided to leave London and his troubles behind?

On the Grand Junction towpath, heading south again, he passed two large, square, water pits and began to wish he had taken advantage of facilities back at the offices. With water pits on his right and the canal on his left Best's urge to urinate became urgent. It was no use, he must find a convenient spot. Maybe he should go back to the pub which overlooked the canal a few yards back? No, it was just too late and too far. The matter was urgent.

He made a dash for the light fringe of trees and bushes which lined the towpath and pushed his way far enough to ensure discretion before giving way. Such relief! But what a dreadful smell! As relief became more complete the smell became more overpowering. Maybe this was a favourite watering-hole but, somehow, the odour was not that of human excrement but something thicker, richer and far more unpleasant. Surely, thought Best, the innocent townie, even rotting vegetation could not smell so vile? Maybe there was a pig farm hereabouts?

Gazing around, still suffused by the lingering glow of satisfaction at a relief mission accomplished, his eyes lit upon a scrap of brown corduroy peeping from the undergrowth a few yards away. At least, that's what it looked like. He smiled, had someone got there too late and been forced to leave their trousers behind as a result? His curiosity aroused he went to investigate. It was then that he found Joseph Minchin. It was not a pleasant sight.

Chapter Thirteen

Anthony Wheeler was a short, rather uncouth lad with a thatch of straw-coloured hair and darting, restless eyes which gave him a, possibly undeserved, shifty appearance. He was seventh on PC Smith's second list of names this time made up of ten of Bertrand's pupil painters. There were more, he had been assured, pupils came and went, but these ten were the most consistent attenders.

If the paintings on the walls of Wheeler's bare attic room were anything to go by, the boy was possessed of a prodigious talent. Even Smith could see that, although he found some a bit too misty and indistinct in places for his taste.

Wheeler's recollection of Matilda proved similar to that of most of the other young men he had spoken to: he found her a pleasant, graceful and extremely pretty but rather shy girl, of much better education and class than the usual run of artists' models. But, despite her obvious attractions, Wheeler claimed he had not made any romantic advances towards her.

'Bertrand protected her like a mother hen. In any case,' he grinned in man-to-man fashion, 'she was spoken for.'

Smith sat up eagerly. So much had been hinted at by the others but never spelled out. 'Was she? Who by?'

The boy was suddenly more alert, and hesitated before replying with a shrug, 'Oh, I dunno that.'

Smith was convinced that he did and cursed himself for his clumsiness in reacting so obviously, yet again. Best wouldn't have done that. He would have pretended only polite interest and maybe even changed the subject and come back to it later, casually, oh so casually, when he had made a friend of the boy. It was so hard to keep an interview going and hold all these things in mind. Well, he must let it pass now and try to go back to the subject later.

As a rather desperate diversion he pretended a great interest in harmless details, such as the times the pupils went for their lessons and how often. What they actually did whilst they were there (most of Bertrand's painting, it seemed to Smith) and how helpful the lessons were to them. He began to get the distinct impression that, to Wheeler, the value of the lessons was largely that of providing contacts which might help him further his career. He admitted as much, eventually, when Smith had chatted him into a form of comradeship of the lower orders against the toffs.

'What you got to understand,' Wheeler explained conspiratorially, his eyes darting about the room as though the whole place was new to him, 'is that some of them are just sons of gentlemen – playing at painting. They gives it all up as soon as they gets their inheritances, or they wants to get married and Papa will only cough up if they toes the line. But', he grinned knowingly, 'with a bit of luck, if I 'elps them to paint now and they see how good I am – they'll remember an' help me later, knowin' that they'll get themselves good pictures into the bargain.' He hesitated, then spread his paint-stained hands. 'Well, that's my plan, anyway. D'you see?'

Smith did. He could not but admire a fellow inhabitant of the bottom of the heap reaching up so determinedly and so deviously for the top. 'Good luck to you,' he grinned, and meant it.

Wheeler laughed at Smith's reaction, slapping his thighs noisily in his mirth. Smith chortled in return.

Encouraged by such comradely applause, Wheeler began to elaborate. 'You see, their parents don't like to see 'em doing this, so it's a sort of rebellion, mostly. Some of 'em mean to keep it up an' they have to be dead devious. Take young Charlie Venables. That's not his real name; he daren't use that, his old man – who's loaded with booty – definitely don't want him to be an artist so Charlie has to use a false name when he goes to classes.'

This time Smith controlled his excitement and slapped his thigh too; so that was why he hadn't been able to trace this Venables – it was a false name. He asked a question, the answer to which did not really interest him.

'Why can't he just go off and be a painter anyway?'

'Well, it's hard to get started, innit? If he can't make it, he'll be in dead trouble.'

'What's his real name then?' Smith asked, still laughing. 'The Prince of Wales?'

They both roared with laughter at this, Wheeler pausing only to wipe his eyes with his grubby sleeve. 'No, no – it's Eddie.'

'Oh, Prince Eddie!'

Both parties collapsed with giggles at this. As they quietened down Smith asked, slightly more seriously, a question to which he really did want to know the answer, 'Eddie what?'

'Oh, I dunno,' exclaimed Wheeler, 'who cares?'

Smith gave him a very direct look and answered quietly but firmly, 'I do.'

It was time, he had decided, to become a policeman again and reel in his catch. Wheeler's eyes suddenly stopped roaming about and he looked uncertainly at Smith. Then he grinned. The young policeman was putting him on again. This time Smith did not return the grin, but keeping his eyes steadily on the boy enquired, 'Are you quite sure you don't know Eddie's full name?'

Wheeler was clearly disconcerted, his eyes once again darting wildly around the room in an attempt to avoid Smith's steady gaze until he could gather his thoughts. But Smith was not going to let that happen.

'This is a very serious business,' he said with every serious fibre in his being. 'Heaven knows what charges may arise from it and, if you withhold evidence from me now, you could be charged with aiding or abetting, or, at the very least, obstructing a police officer in the execution of his duty. Your gentry wouldn't want anything to do with you then, would they? Your career would be finished. Don't forget, you've got no rich daddy to fall back on.'

The message hit home. Smith had correctly divined that the one thing in life that really meant anything to Wheeler was his painting. But, obviously, he felt he couldn't betray his friend without at least a show of loyalty. 'But I don't know, honest. Eddie's all he's ever said – 'e goes on about his father wanting him to go into the business . . . '

'Where does he live, this Eddie?' Smith cut in coldly.

'I dunno, honest.'

'This girl might be dead,' snapped Smith with icy bluntness.

All the bravado evaporated. The boy was at sea, eyes everywhere. Smith knew he had him. He pinned him down with a glare. 'Murdered!'

The lad began to stutter, 'I know – North London – I think that was it. No, I know, near Regent's Park, somewhere. He used to walk there and paint.'

'St John's Wood, was it?'

'That's it. That's it! St John's Wood.' His relief was palpable. He was off the hook but had not told tales. Well, not really.

But Smith was not finished. 'And,' he said softly, 'it is him who had spoken for Matilda?' The boy was riveted by Smith's icy gaze. 'Isn't it?'

Wheeler, fish-like, opened and closed his mouth.

'Say it!' shouted Smith. 'Just say it!'

'Yes,' the boy whispered, 'it was him.'

'And his name?' Smith almost spat the words.

'Eddie, Eddie Van Ellen.' The lad looked about to cry.

I'm learning, thought Smith.

Joseph Minchin's body was suspended at an angle face down on the low bushes. Head near the ground, feet in the air, and right arm outstretched as though to ward off a blow. Leaves had died off and fallen from the undergrowth leaving a mesh of bare branches which afforded a good view of what was left of the body. But it was of little use apart from convincing Best that this was the body of Joseph Minchin. He could see no evidence of a wound. Holding his handkerchief to his nose and mouth he tried hard not to be sick, but failed miserably.

Oh, God what a mess this was going to be, he realized, after he had got over the initial shock and revulsion and began hurrying back in the direction of the junction buildings. Now he had the task of obtaining the services of the local police and doctor – without arousing too much local interest.

He must also inform Cheadle via an electric telegraph message written in language which explained to the Chief Inspector what had happened, but did not alert the telegraphist. The clerk, like so many of his kind, would doubtless have direct and profitable links with the Press but, in this backwater, little opportunity to benefit from them. But inform Cheadle quickly, that was essential. He needed reinforcements – fast.

His haste and worried look were attracting attention. With some effort he slowed his pace and assumed a less concerned expression. The last thing he needed was hordes of curious sightseers tramping all over the scene before he had a chance to look at it properly. He had already taken some notes, before nausea again overtook him, but he wanted a better look around and under the body.

'Oh no, we ain't got none of *those*,' said the local constable with some satisfaction when Best asked about getting their detectives to the scene. 'We just do it all ourselves, like,' he added, managing with his half-smile, to make the whole concept of detection appear an unnecessary, uppity idea.

Of course you do, thought Best bitterly. Then you call in the Yard when the bird is well flown and all the evidence has been destroyed. Then you put obstacles in our way and encourage the local community to thwart us and treat us as enemies. Then you can blame us when we can't find the culprit.

Best knew he shouldn't anticipate trouble, but should be looking on the bright side, counting his advantages. For example, it was a great advantage that he was there at the outset, indeed that he had found the body. His knowledge of the case and the Force having no detectives at all were also blessings. Being called in when they had their own detectives could be worst of all.

He began forming his plan of action. He would offer, oh so tactfully, to take over the investigation, using his foreknowledge of the case and characters and its connection with the one they were already handling, to justify his immediate control. He would be modest, helpful and make it clear that he did not assume that his position of control was inevitable. Moreover, he would acknowledge that he would be utterly dependent on, and extremely grateful for, the local knowledge of the Hertfordshire officers. He needn't have worried. When Captain Robertson, the divisional superintendent, arrived from Hemel Hempstead, he proved a reasonable man in charge of an overstretched division. Indeed, he confided with some disgust, the whole county Force numbered only 117 men. The fact that the Hertfordshire Police were well established helped as well. No beginners' inferiority complex niggling its senior officers. And it was sufficiently close to London to make contact with the Metropolitan Police more usual and less threatening.

Superintendent Robertson was only too willing to let his constables guard the scene and leave the rest to the Yard man subject, of course, to permission from his chief constable. Blessedly, that officer was not only on the best of terms with the Commissioner of the Metropolitan Police but was also situated miles away in Hertford which delayed the seeking of permission and gave Best merciful breathing space. Panic over. Now to work.

Minchin's twisted body had been lifted on to a board which, in turn, had been placed on a hand ambulance and spirited away along a pathway which took it a long way round to the village, but avoided alerting those on the canal towpath. But such news travels like lightning and Best knew it was only a matter of time before the deluge of attention would begin. Nonetheless, before returning to search the area again, he had to contact Cheadle. He spent precious time writing and rewriting his message trying to find a way to say that he had found his quarry, but that he was dead.

In the end he could think of nothing better than: *Quarry found, dcd. Taking charge, please send assistance. Letter follows*. He was optimistic that Cheadle would realize what 'dcd' meant and the telegraph operator wouldn't, although he didn't hold out much hope of that. In any case, a telegraph addressed to Scotland Yard would doubtless put the man on full alert. Maybe he should just be straightforward and say, 'Minchin found dead'. Otherwise, he would be accused of being fancy – and even obtuse, if Cheadle knew what that meant. Perhaps he shouldn't say 'taking charge' until he had the chief constable's permission?

'Can I help you?' asked a vaguely familiar melancholy voice. Best looked up to see Traffic Manager Albert Thornley, framed in the doorway, 'I've heard the news,' Thornley said, and sighed. He looked more worried than ever, as well he might. But what on earth what was he doing here?

The traffic manager sensed Best's puzzlement, 'I came up to see if I might trace up Minchin,' he offered apologetically, avoiding Best's incredulous eye. The man is well aware that that is precisely what I'm doing, thought Best, and he had made sure he got here before I did. In fact, he must have come by train! Small wonder he looked abashed. Curious wording that, too, 'I came up' not 'I was sent up'.

'I hear it was suicide?'

'Seems so.' Best was not going to be drawn.

'That must be a relief – not too much work to do.'

'Oh, I don't know about that,' said Best casually. 'In a case like this – got to be sure.' He paused and, without attempting to take the edge off his voice, asked, 'You been here long?'

'Oh, just a few hours.' Thornley shifted his weight from one foot to the other under the Sergeant's icy gaze.

Not prepared to be specific, obviously. What was going on?

'He *was* our employee,' explained Thornley stiffly, 'and, of course, we felt it our duty to check what happened to him.'

Touching, that, answered Best's unrelenting stare.

'And the company want to be of as much assistance to the police as possible, naturally.'

Now, he really is lying, thought Best.

'I've been asking around the village. Just see if he knew anyone here, or if any stranger had been seen hereabouts,'

Thornley added lamely. The man was embarrassed, as he might well be. He knew that asking around was exactly what Best had intended to do. But then again he certainly could use the help of a man who wielded some authority hereabouts.

Thornley could see to it that the telegraph was despatched quickly, get him a list of the canal company men likely to be at Marsworth on the night in question, help in parrying reporters, and find some trusty men to assist in guarding the scene. What he did *not* want Thornley to do was to accompany him when he went back to examine it – which he must do now, before complete darkness fell. Then he realized the futility of that – if the man was in any way involved in Minchin's demise he would already have done what he had to do to cover his tracks. Nonetheless, Best gave Thornley enough work to keep him busy elsewhere and returned, alone. He was pleased to note that the local constable had carried out his guard duty discreetly and well and had not succumbed to the temptation to trample round the scene. Doubtless, the lingering, pungent smell had helped dissuade him.

When removing the body, the cause of death became apparent. Not only was Minchin's outstretched hand loosely grasping an open razor but his wrists had been slashed and beneath them were pools of dried-up blood.

Suicide.

It looked quite conclusive but, just to be on the safe side, Best now went back to go over the ground again, raking through the broken branches, his handkerchief once again clamped to his mouth and nose. Something might have fallen from Minchin's pocket, or there could be a letter and, although everything pointed to it, he mustn't just presume that Minchin had killed himself. He had to keep an open mind. It seemed an odd place to go to end one's life – but, then again, maybe only to a landsman like himself. These canals and their surrounds were the boatmen's roads and streets.

But Minchin wasn't a regular boatman. Maybe the compulsion just came over him and he headed for the nearest spot. Would it have been light enough, Best wondered? As a townie, he took little notice of the moon's waxes and wanes but he knew it became very dark in the country on moonless nights. He must find out whether it had shone that night and if the sky had been clear or cloudy. But then, he mimed the movements, you wouldn't need any light to find your own wrists. He continued his search, wavering only when maggots rolled slowly down the slimy leaves as he lifted them with his stick, before plopping on to the ground.

He had all but given up when he spotted something in the soft, peaty earth he had now revealed with his stick; a boot print just below where Minchin's head had rested. What's more, it was a deep and definite print with a clear, hobnail pattern. Obviously, the man had trodden around a deal before he did the deed, quite a natural thing to do thought Best, who couldn't imagine cutting himself deliberately under any circumstances. He cursed himself for not noting what Minchin's boots had been like. He made a note to get hold of them. Meanwhile, he had better get some plaster of Paris to preserve the print, just to be on the safe side.

One thing was certain, if anyone else had had a hand in the death of Joseph Minchin he would have been heavily bloodstained. But who would have noticed in the dark? He must ask Thornley to check. Ah, no, better not do that: he was no longer sure about Thornley.

Chapter Fourteen

The once-prosperous village of Braunston was well past its prime when Best strode along its High Street just as the first chill of winter began to grip the air. But it still seemed a passing pleasant place to the Sergeant, strung out as it was along the ridge of the Northamptonshire uplands.

Unlike some canalside villages, which appeared to be just stuck around the waterway to serve its purposes and that of commerce, Braunston had a proper centre. It also had a small, triangular village green, a school and a surprisingly large and imposing church with a tall spire visible for miles around. The houses were a pleasing mixture of styles and materials from mellow, golden stone to red brick.

The boatmen had described the disastrous effect of the coming of the railways on this historic coach and canal crossroads so he was aware that many of the dwellings he admired were empty. The inhabitants had either emigrated or gone to where the prospect of work seemed better. That was exactly what Mary Elizabeth Jones had done when she lost her job with the Chambers family at Manley Hall.

One of the few ways of life still thriving in the area was that of the gentry. Their considerable presence was due largely to the pleasant countryside, the abundance of foxes and the generosity of a grateful William the Conqueror who had doled out parcels of the land to his nobles. Ironically, the convenience of railway travel had brought new money in as well.

It was with one of these families, the Chambers at Manley Hall, that the fair and lovely Mary Elizabeth Jones had obtained a good position: first as a parlour-maid, then a lady's maid – quite a leap for a poor miner's daughter. But then, not only had Mary Elizabeth been remarkably delicate-looking for someone from her background, but she had been better educated than most, having been taught to read and write at the village school – unlike her elder sister Liza who now sat opposite Best.

'Our mother died and someone had to look after the family while my father was out working down the mines,' she explained. Liza was a sturdier, stronger-boned version of her sister with mousy brown, rather than fair, hair and an air of sadness not due solely, Best reckoned, to the fate of her sister but also an awareness of chances of happiness probably lost for ever for duty's sake.

'There was eight of us and I wanted them to do as well so they could get on – and to get away from all this.' She gazed bleakly around at the cold, bare room then down at her own worn dress and pinny. Best wished he had dirtied his shoes a little and worn a rough necktie. His immaculate appearance was not only an affront amidst such dire poverty, but it was making this good, simple woman self-conscious, more aware and ashamed of her shabby surroundings and clothes.

'Mary Elizabeth was . . . is the next eldest.' She smiled sadly. 'The princess we used to call her. Mind you, she used to teach me some reading and writing when we had time – so I can read – just a little.' She blushed at her claims, her reddened hands grasping each other in support. 'She was very patient with me, she was.'

'Was it her first job – the one at Manley Hall?'

'Oh no, Mr Best. First off she worked as a barmaid at a pub down on the green. I got to say I didn't like that but there was nothing else for her and the landlord looked after her.

Then Mrs Chambers saw how nicely she handed out the stirrup cup one New Year's Day and took a shine to her. Took her on. She loved it, did Mary, fair blossomed. Mrs Chambers gave her some of her old clothes and, oh, she did look so lovely in them when she went out walking on her afternoon off.'

'Why did she want to leave?'

'Oh she didn't: she was made to.' Liza's eyes filled and she clenched her strong hands. 'She was too pretty, you see, and Mr Chambers began going after her. Mary didn't know what to do, did she? Kept trying to dodge him like, but it was no use an' then Mrs Chambers caught him trying to kiss her.'

A familiar story.

'So she was told to leave.'

'Yes, right away. "Pack your box this minute!", Mrs Chambers shouted at her, didn't she, and "Get out of this house. We're respectable here". That's what she said.' The injustice of it still burned. 'Mrs Chambers blamed her for "tempting Mr Chambers", that's what she said, didn't she, an' Mary knew right off that she wouldn't get another job in these parts after that. But the butler, he could see what was going on, an' he took pity on her and gives her a reference and two addresses to try for in London.'

'When was that?'

'Back in March. She went down to London on one of the boats.'

Best's expression must have shown surprise that such a pretty girl should be put on a boat on her own for Liza said quickly, 'That's how we all travel, it's natural to us you see, and we've all got relatives and friends on the boats. She went down on *Nella Queen* with her Aunt Hester and Uncle George.'

'Did Mr Chambers know where she was going?'

Liza looked surprised, such an idea obviously had not crossed her mind. 'I don't know.'

'Could the reference have been on his say-so, d'you think?'

Her eyes widened. 'I s'pose it's possible, Mr Best.' She frowned thinking back for clues. 'I s'pose you might 'ave something there. I never thought of that.' She paused. 'I should 'ave done,' she said sadly, 'I should 'ave done.'

Best's heart bled for the woman whose eyes were pleading with him to tell her that the body found in the canal was not that of her beloved sister. He'd been putting off the evil moment, partly for practicality's sake. She had been a willing participant. But now they both knew it was time to stop and face it. With a sigh, Best reached into his inside pocket and brought out a paper bag containing the victim's petticoat. The instant she saw it tears began to pour unheeded down Liza's face. She sat immobile, transfixed by the pretty, lace-trimmed garment. Best longed to hug her, to comfort her, she seemed so desperately alone. But it was too awkward while she sat so he leaned over and patted her hand, held it and whispered, 'I'm so sorry.'

The gesture seemed to undo her completely and a howl of anguish came from the back of her throat, followed by sobs so heartrending Best hoped he would never hear the like again.

'My baby! Oh my baby!' she cried out, and sobbed and sobbed.

When the worst had subsided Best handed her his last clean handkerchief.

'I'm sorry, I did not mean for that . . . ' She got up, looking round desperately, trying to compose herself, but, breaking down again and grasping the back of the chair, she leaned over and howled, 'Oh, Mary Elizabeth! My darling girl!'

This time Best followed his instincts and put his arms around the grieving woman and let her sob her heart out on the sleeve of his best plaid jacket.

After a while, he said quietly and slowly, 'Now Liza, we must find out who did this.' She nodded helplessly. 'I'm going to go off for a couple of hours, so you can recover a little and tell who you have to.' She held his handkerchief to her lips to stifle the fresh sobs this thought brought on. 'Then, I'll come back and talk to you again because, you see,' – he grasped her hand tightly – 'I need your help. Without you, I can't find the person who did it.' He paused. 'Is that all right?'

She nodded wordlessly and finally managed to gasp out, 'You're a good man. She should have found someone like you.'

Best spent the two hours eating a steak pie and downing a pint of strong local ale at The Dog and Gun, opposite the school on the village green. After attending the opening of Minchin's inquest, Best had seized the opportunity to continue up to Braunston before it resumed again two days later. Now, as he ate and drank he read the letters from Cheadle and Smith which he'd collected from the canal office. The first contained more or less what he had expected, the second shook him.

By the time he returned to Liza she had dried her eyes, tidied her hair, washed, dried and ironed his handkerchief, lit a fire in the grate, and regained some self control, but it was still a fragile thing. To help her retain it Best refrained from mentioning anything that had gone before and adopted a kind, but dispassionate and businesslike manner.

The fire, poor as it was, was particularly welcome on this increasingly chilly day. Coal, he had been told, was one thing that was quite cheap hereabouts, due to the canal trade. Even the poorest could gather the dust. But, he was painfully aware that she would not have lit it just for herself, it was the one way she could be hospitable. He sat on the right-hand side of the grate, in a wheel-back chair which leaned to the left where one leg was shorter, facing Liza perched on a scrubbed but dilapidated kitchen chair. She began to explain how – when she had last heard – her sister had got a job as a chamber-maid, quite quickly, and was doing well.

'When was that.'

'September, 'bout the middle.' She held out a blue envelope from the small pile in her lap.

Best noticed it did not carry a stamp.

'How did it come? By canal?'

She nodded. 'Aunt and Uncle usually brought them up, but they don't always get down to London so sometimes one of the company men on the fly run would bring them – quicker and more regular, you see.'

'And who brought this one?'

'Charles Baxton.'

The skipper of the *Tilbury* who had been killed. Best sat forward in his chair causing it to rock. 'They knew each other well?'

'Oh, no.' She shook her head. 'I don't think so. Not as I knows, anyway.'

'Did he always bring them?'

'Oh no, no. Different person each time, mostly. Anyone who happened to be on the next fly run, I suppose, an' who could be trusted.'

'Did they have money in them?'

She nodded sadly. 'Sometimes, when she could, when she could. She wanted to keep the children in school as well, but it's hard enough just to feed them now.' She looked embarrassed by what she had just said and just so that he'd not think she was asking for charity, added proudly, 'But we'll manage, somehow.'

How much do you eat? Best wondered, noticing just how painfully thin she was. 'So it was a different man each time?'

'Most times, yes. She just left the letters in the Grand Junction office.'

Best tried not to show any quickened interest. 'Who would that be with?'

'Oh, it was all proper. She left them with the gaffer there. His name was' – she struggled to recall it – 'I dunno. Albert something – something like prickles . . . '

'Albert Thornley.'

'That's it. That's him.'

'She was friendly with him?'

'Not special, I don't think. He just did her a kindness – and me. I used to write back' – she looked down at her hands – 'best I could, 'course, and they left them in the office.'

Best nodded. 'Did she mention anyone else there?'

'No. Not as I recall. She only told me his name because he gave permission and that. But you can see yourself.' She held out the rest of the bundle of letters.

Best took them. 'Thank you. I'd be obliged if I could keep them for a while, Miss Jones, in case I can find any useful information in them.'

The idea clearly upset her, tears jumping into her eyes as she agreed. 'Yes, Mr Best, of course you can.'

'I'll guard them with my life,' he promised. Then he fired the last and most potentially upsetting question at her. 'Why did you not tell us sooner that she was missing?'

'She wasn't! Not that I knew! She was happy and well.' Tears spilled over. 'Even when we heard about the girl being found in the canal, I never thought . . . there was no reason.' Tears were coming fast now. Best handed her his newly-laundered handkerchief. 'It weren't until I was told about the petticoats with the hearts that I thought it might be . . . ' She broke down, then.

'Just one last question. Where did she work?'

'At Grantham House – in . . . in Mary something,' she sobbed.

'Marylebone?'

She looked confused. 'I suppose that's it, something like that.'

Oh well, at least it wasn't St John's Wood, Best thought, as he stepped back on to the High Street. Shabby children, mostly boys, released from the school were running towards him shouting and laughing. But it wasn't far off either.

At first, Van Ellen attempted to be his usual implacable self and Smith began by politely requesting to talk to the younger son, Eddie Van Ellen. But when Van Ellen airily dismissed the request, saying that the boy was out and anyway too busy, Smith suddenly found himself becoming startlingly firm and implacable in return.

'Is your son in the house at this moment?' he demanded of a pinker-than-usual Van Ellen.

'No.'

'Then I wish to see his room.' As he spoke he stood up and moved forward.

Van Ellen was taken unawares. 'But ... but ... '

'Lead the way, please,' he said commandingly and Van Ellen did. He's holding something back, Smith thought to himself when his astonishment subsided. That's why he gave way so easily, he's confused.

Eddie's room was probably much the same as any other in the house, but it was clear by the rigidity of his bearing and the pink spots on his cheeks, that its contents had earned the disapproval of his father. It must be the pictures, Smith concluded. He could see no other reason. Two were views of dockland in the same vague style as those he had seen in Anthony Wheeler's attic. Another, resting against the wall, was a rather amateurish portrait of a young woman wearing pink, but it was impossible to see her face for the violent slashes of red which had obliterated it.

Smith was suddenly aware of something other than disapproval in Van Ellen's demeanour – fear. 'How long has your son been gone, sir?' he enquired peremptorily.

'I don't know what you mean . . . '

'You know exactly what I mean. And I must remind you that this is a very serious matter. Now I ask you again, sir, how long has your son been away?'

The man hesitated, then crumpled. With a look of utter defeat which astonished Smith, he muttered, 'Since last Tuesday.'

Five days.

'Where is he?'

To Smith's further astonishment the man began to cry quite silently, the tears welling up, spilling over and being allowed to flow unchecked down his still face as he stood, an immobile picture of abject misery.

'Just tell me, sir?' said the PC more gently.

'I don't know!' Sobs began to rack the man's pink, plump face making him look more like an overgrown baby than ever. 'I just don't know!'

'He didn't tell anyone where he was going?'

The man shook his head, unable to speak.

'He is missing from home, in fact?'

'I shouldn't have been so hard on him . . . I should have . . . '

The PC ignored this and asked bluntly, 'Wouldn't he have told his mother or his sister even?' Smith couldn't imagine going anywhere without telling his mother.

He shook his head. 'They're as distressed as I am!'

Smith nodded thoughtfully to hide a sudden lack of resolve. What should he ask next? To cover his confusion he opened the wardrobe door. Then it came to him. 'Did he take many clothes with him?'

They both knew this was the most serious question of all. Suicides did not need hairbrushes nor a change of clothes. 'No,' said Van Ellen. He had difficulty in getting the words out but eventually said in a small, quiet voice, 'None. And I understand that it seems he did not even take his toiletries.'

'Would he have much money?'

'Some cash, but not a great deal and, the terrible thing is . . . ' The man could scarcely speak but Smith motioned him on. 'He hasn't drawn any money from his bank account since!'

'Right, I want you and every other member of the household to tell me everything, and I mean everything, about your son that they can think of.'

Van Ellen was gathering himself together as best he could. 'Of course.'

'We will do our best to find him.' Smith patted the man's hand suddenly feeling much older. He still couldn't get over the change in Van Ellen. All signs of the arrogant man of power had gone. He merely nodded, gratefully. Neither made any mention of what might happen to the son should they find him alive, and his beloved permanently removed from the scene in as savage a manner as she had been from the painting propped against the wall.

Chapter Fifteen

The first thing Best saw as he climbed up from the towpath to the White Lion Public House at Marsworth, was the bulky figure of Cheadle. It wasn't just the man's presence which surprised Best but his garb.

The Chief Inspector was dressed as for the country, a symphony in brown. Gone were the regulation dark frock coat and trousers, stiff collar and top hat. In their place, a Norfolk jacket and plus-fours fashioned from a marmalade tweed. This ensemble was topped off by a pale chocolate-coloured bowler.

Alongside Cheadle, like a cast of characters lining up in a play to take a bow, were Albert Thornley, Sam Grealey, and a slight, sad figure whom Best took to be Mrs Minchin. She wore a shabby but neat black dress relieved by touches of cheap white lace and, at her neck, a tiny jet brooch. Around her shoulders, but scarcely protection against the raw morning air, was a light woollen shawl. Indeed, she was shivering. But, as Smith had noticed, there was a dignity about the way the woman held herself and in the turn of her fair head.

Grealey greeted him like a long-lost brother despite the fact that he now knew him to be a policeman. Cheadle and Thornley acknowledged him with brief nods. The resumed inquest on the sudden death of Joseph Minchin was to take place in an upstairs room of the pub. Best had been to several such rural inquests but none as close to the murder scene – scarcely a hundred yards – and as appropriate as this one. The White Lion overlooked the canal and was a familiar part of the waterway scenery and life.

Best was puzzled by Cheadle's presence. Why had he come all this way for an inquest at which the verdict was almost a foregone conclusion: suicide while the balance of the mind was disturbed. Why this sudden interest?

Another strange thing he noticed, apart from his chief's metamorphosis into a country gentleman, was the man's oddly benign behaviour. The probable explanation dawned slowly. It must be the presence of the grieving Mrs Minchin for whom, it soon transpired, nothing was too good. When they partook of a light lunch she must have the choicest cuts of meat and the most comfortable, least draughty seat in the inglenook.

This new vision of an old warhorse was startling but, never having seen the Chief Inspector in the presence of ladies, it was impossible to judge whether the confirmed bachelor extended this extravagant solicitude to Mrs Minchin alone or to all of her sex. Perhaps the man was merely being kind? The very thought bemused Best and made him smile to himself.

Whatever, it was it was good to see the shabby, stricken woman warming to the man's elaborate and overdone attentions. Indeed, when she smiled gratefully at Cheadle in thanks for one particular nicety, Best glimpsed remnants of an attractive woman shining forth, but was brought up sharp when she turned her head. The translucence of the skin of her cheek was just like that of Emma in her last days.

He realized he hadn't seen Grealey in the presence of women either and that sight also proved to be something of an eye-opener.

His manner was preening. Indeed, he managed to give the impression that, should he be interested, no other man would stand a chance in his handsome and virile presence. He was probably right there, but it was soon plain he wasn't interested in the pale and wispy Mrs Minchin. Probably not to his lusty taste. The sturdy and peach-like barmaid apparently was and, while he was sensible enough not to openly flirt with her in such circumstances, Grealey's eyes followed her everywhere and caught hers as she bent over to lay their places. He managed to murmur lasciviously to his friend Best as to what he could do were he in extremely close quarters with the young lady.

En route to Marsworth, Best had reread the letter from Smith giving him the amazing news that the Van Ellen boy was Matilda's sweetheart. It made him itch to be back in London to confront the Van Ellens and he worried whether Smith was experienced enough to handle the matter properly. What would he do if Van Ellen refused to answer his questions? Best hesitated to bring the matter up with Cheadle. Now that the victim's identity had been established he may not think they should still be pursuing the matter. But to Best's mind, Matilda was still a woman missing in mysterious circumstances and maybe, who knows, another victim of the canal murderer.

The letters sent home by Mary Elizabeth had also provided illuminating reading on his return journey to Marsworth. Alongside many exclamations as to what a big, frightening but exciting city London was, were details regarding her life as a chamber-maid, which appeared quite hard, and a complete run-down on her fellow servants who, apparently, were all in thrall to one man. Not, of course, the head of the family but the purple-cheeked Mr Bates, the butler. A man certainly worth talking to, Best thought.

Now he was faced with another letter, handed to him by Cheadle with whom he had gone into a private huddle. This letter was sensational. It was from Minchin and, in it, he confessed to the murder of Mary Elizabeth, or at least, appeared to do so. *I am guilty of the killing,* announced a large, wavering black scrawl which obviously had taken some effort to execute. Then there was a signature, and that was that.

'Looks like he did commit suicide then,' murmured Best.

'Looks like,' said Cheadle. 'She says it's his handwriting.' He nodded towards Mrs Minchin.

'How'd she take it?'

'She don't believe it,' he answered bluntly. 'Says he never had no other woman but her.'

They exchanged knowing glances.

'I must say,' offered Best thoughtfully, 'the idea did seem a bit strange to me. I mean, I know I only saw him briefly ...'

This was the wrong thing to say. Cheadle gave him an icy look. 'We all knows about that, don't we, Sergeant?' He looked over at Grealey, still engaged on his furthering of the barmaid quest and looking mighty pleased with himself in the process. There was no sign of his twitch. 'Was him that told you that, weren't it?'

'Yes.'

Cheadle voiced it for them both. 'Looks a bit like the pot calling the kettle, don't it?'

Best nodded. 'It does,' adding carefully, 'but, maybe, if Minchin wasn't very successful with women he would take rejection harder?'

Cheadle grunted with, Best sensed, a hint of embarrassment. Oh dear, maybe he was getting too near home. 'Well, anyway,' shrugged the Chief Inspector, holding up the confessional letter, 'it looks like it were him, don't it?'

It occurred to Best that they only had Mrs Minchin's word that it was her husband's handwriting but, somehow, as he followed his chief's besotted gaze, he felt that this would not be the right moment to voice that doubt so contented himself with a brief, 'It does that.' It suddenly occurred to him that the sight of Mrs Minchin and Grealey so studiously avoiding each other was an odd one.

Minchin and Grealey might not have been close friends, but they had been workmates.

Cheadle, however, had not taken complete leave of his senses. 'Bit pat, though, the note and all, ain't it?' he muttered finally.

The inquest hearing had gone much as Best expected. A procession of witnesses, starting with himself as the finder of the body, then the surgeon saying, in more complicated terms, that the cause of death was loss of blood due to the injuries to the throat and wrists. Canal workmen followed, describing where and when they had last seen Joseph Minchin and what mental condition he had been in at that time. Morose was the general opinion, but that, it seemed, was his normal demeanour.

That the deceased was a possible suspect in a murder case was only touched upon. Before proceedings had commenced, Cheadle had seen the coroner and persuaded him that any divulging of detail would hamper the enquiry. He'd asked him to accept in court a statement begging the court's indulgence regarding the information about this matter. The coroner had been reluctant, knowing that would mean another adjournment. Coroners could be very jealous of their authority and status, but Cheadle had flattered the man, hinting that while he had the chief constable on his side the police chief's word was as naught compared to that of the coroner. Thus it was that not even the confession note was mentioned.

Outside, the light had begun to fade to a golden glow which reflected into the water and off the boats and their reflections. The effect was dreamlike and so peaceful in contrast to all this talk of violent death. If only Helen Franks could see that, sighed Best to himself. He must lose no time in telling her that the victim was not her sister. That would give her some respite.

The final witness appeared as the pub lamps were being lit. It was evident that Mrs Minchin did not see her husband in quite the light his colleagues had done. He was a kind man, she declared, and a good husband and father – brought down by his love of gambling. And he only did that to try to better their lot. The heat of the room brought an appealing flush in her fair cheeks and, as she spoke about his increasing worries about money, she stressed her words with graceful hand movements in the air. The effect, as the darkness deepened in the windows behind her, was hypnotic. Cheadle and Grealey particularly were transfixed. What was it, thought Best. The grace? The femininity? Or the self-possession – so odd in someone of her station in life? The accent was clearly cockney and her vocabulary limited, but the voice was low and pleasant. Whatever it was, she was clearly one of those people that the more you saw of her, the more she intrigued you. A bit like Helen Franks, thought Best suddenly, and was irritated at himself for allowing her re-entry into his subconscious twice in ten minutes. I miss her, he thought miserably, before dragging his mind back to the present.

Had Minchin's problems been only monetary? Grealey's hungry eyes watching her made him wonder again. Or had his wife caused him some difficulty? Driven him into the arms of other women who he was unable to shake off when he tired of them?

The coroner was just beginning to thank Mrs Minchin for attending to give evidence when she held up her hand gently to stop him.

'There's something else I fink I should tell you,' she murmured in a voice so low that Best had to strain to hear her.

'What's that, my dear?' the coroner's voice boomed around the suddenly hushed room.

She drew a graceful arc with her right arm to point at the table containing the exhibits. 'That ain't his razor.'

Chapter Sixteen

The crew of the *Mary Louise* sat, razors in hand, on the grass beside the canal. All the cut-throats had proved to be of exactly the same make and pattern and all had handles of imitation ebony – just like the one which had cut Minchin's throat. Hardly surprising. It was a common make and they all bought from the same canalside shops.

Yet the man's own razor, his wife claimed, had an ivory handle inscribed with his initials. She didn't know whether it was in the bundle of his belongings which had been returned to her. That was back in London and she had not opened it. Couldn't bring herself to, yet.

'This is just what we need,' Best said to Cheadle, 'another murder.'

'Still, doesn't have to be murder, you know,' Cheadle said mildly. 'He could have picked up someone else's razor – easy done – these blokes live on top of each other. Or maybe he didn't care. Sudden decision to end it all – grabs any handy razor.'

Best was beginning to find this newly benign Chief Inspector disconcerting. Was he going totally soft? He hadn't even berated Best for not checking whether the razor found by the body was Minchin's. Even seemed to look pleased about the whole thing. Because it would give him an excuse to see Mrs Minchin again? And what on earth had he been doing with his hair? Normally a strong but dull dark brown and a bit lifeless, it looked newly shiny and puffed up.

'An' we got the confession, ain't we? Topping himself before we could do the job. *Looks* like suicide, don't it?'

Best wished he'd make up his mind. 'Looks like,' he agreed, thinking again that they only had Mrs Minchin's word for the handwriting. But then it was Mrs Minchin who had thrown doubt on a suicide verdict. What was going on?

'The thing we got to ask ourselves,' muttered Cheadle, 'is why would anyone want to kill Joseph Minchin? We got to look at the picture from the other side, d'you see?'

Best was a bit sick of pictures . . . and artists . . . and models and —

'People he owed money to?' he suggested.

'Wouldn't get the money at all then, would they?'

Best shrugged. 'But it would teach others a lesson?'

'Mebbe, mebbe. But it's a bit complicated coming all the way up here to do it, innit? Seems a bit out of proportion, don't it? Can't see our East End shysters coming out here in the country. They'd get lost ten minutes from Seven Dials. Stand out like sore thumbs an' all. 'Course we don't know 'ow *much* he owed, but I can't see as it could be that much, d'you?'

'To shift the blame for the murder onto him, then? The confession could be a forgery.'

'She was pretty certain. No question in her mind.'

Best decided to avoid any suggestion that the wonderful Mrs Minchin could be lying. 'Could be a good forgery?' he suggested instead. But then, when he thought about it, why, when it was she who had blown the whistle on the razor? He felt exhausted and totally confused.

'Mebbe, but these blokes can scarcely write their names anyway. Can't see them forging someone else's script.'

'*If* it was a boatman,' said Best. 'But you're right, anyone else would stick out on the canals. I certainly did.'

Cheadle grinned. 'I hears they gave you a new handle.'

Best had heard that too. 'I know, Shiny Boots.' He waited until Cheadle stopped guffawing, allowing himself a slight smile so as not to appear too thin-skinned. 'What I can't make out if it was murder, is how someone could overpower a strong, fit, wide-awake man and cut his wrists. Minchin wasn't muscular but he was wiry and strong. They all are, doing that kind of work.'

'More than one assailant?' suggested Cheadle.

'Possible, ' said Best, 'But the scene wasn't *that* trampled about.'

'If it *was* murder,' agreed his Chief Inspector. 'By the way, Sayers has made an arrest.'

'He's solved the Thames murder!' exclaimed Best excitedly.

'No, not exactly. Found the Limehouse woman's body in their garden. Her old man's coughed up.'

Best was having another go at the boatmen but was getting nowhere. No clues as to Minchin's apparent intentions that night, or as to whom the strange razor belonged. All on board still had their own but then, they would, wouldn't they, if they had any sense?

'So there is nothing you can tell me that you think would be any help?' he asked the gathered crew. 'He was quite normal that night?'

They all nodded.

'Oh yeah,' said the skipper.

''Part from his gripes,' said the lad.

There was a short silence while Best absorbed this new idea. 'His what?'

'His gripes.'

'His complaints, you mean?'

'Na. Belly gripes.'

'He was sick!' exclaimed Best looking around angrily. 'Why didn't anybody tell me this before?'

'Didn't fink it mattered,' muttered the lad, avoiding the policeman's glare.

'Nobody asked us,' put in the skipper, sulkily. 'Just says was he cheerful or what?'

'Well he wouldn't be cheerful if he was sick, would he?' said the Sergeant testily. He paused to get a grip on his temper. No point in making them button up again. 'Was he sick bad?' he enquired more mildly.

'Hard to say. Taken sudden like. Looked a bit grassy – then rushed off.'

'And no one went to find him when he didn't come back?'

They looked at each other and shook their heads. 'Skipper was in bed, off his shift, Harry was seeing to the locks and I was aboard. 'Course, we looked later when he didn't seem to be coming back, but it was dark and we couldn't find him. Thought he'd just got fed up and gawn orff. Happens.'

'Was anyone else ill?'

They shook their heads.

'Did you all eat the same things?'

They all nodded. 'Yeah,' said the skipper.

'Did he get anything to eat from anyone else?'

'Dunno,' said the skipper, looking at the men who all shrugged.

The lad grinned. 'There was this nice smell coming from his mate's boat.'

'His mate?' Best tried to curb his impatience and stop his voice from rising as he said, '*What mate?*'

'On one of the company boats going south. I saw him talking to one of them ...'

'Which boat? What name?'

The lad shook his head. 'Can't remember ...'

'*Try!*'

They looked at him in wonderment. 'You think he was poisoned?' the skipper laughed. 'Easy enough up here, I'll grant you.'

'What d'you mean? Easy?'

He gestured towards the bank. 'They're full of poison, them – if you know which ones to look for.'

'What? Berries? Like deadly-nightshade? Foxgloves? Or toadstools?' asked new country-boy Best, excitedly. Being ill, *that* would have made Minchin easier to kill.

'Oh, aye, toadstools, an' berries, an' roots, an' leaves, an' flowers as well. Even the pretty ones, lily of the valley, jasmine, cowbane – you just got to know which, and how much, that's all.' A sly look came over his face.

'And boatmen do know?'

'Oh, aye, a lot of them any rates.'

They were all grinning at him now. Best felt adrift in a strange land of secret practices and different laws.

'What was it you smelled cooking? A stew?'

'Mebbe.' The lad thought about it a bit. 'Nah, it were more like grilled meat – put on sticks or spikes an' done on a fire.'

'On the boat?'

'Dunno,' he shrugged, glancing at the skipper warily, 'mebbe by the side.'

Best began to deflate, grilled meat didn't seem very promising for passing on poison.

'Yew,' said the skipper suddenly reading his thoughts, 'that'd do it.'

Not knowing which poison, if any, may have been administered, all Best could do was to delay Minchin's burial for further investigation of stomach contents and see if he could find sufficient traces of vomit which he could get as a specimen. But he realized that time was against him.

'You try to remember which boat the man was on,' he urged the lad, adding, 'There's a good reward in it for you, if you do,' hoping the commissioner would cough up. 'I'll see you when you get to London.'

Meanwhile, he had some jobs for Smith to work on in London. If he got writing now, he could make the evening post.

Smith was following up yet another list of names; those given him by the now humble Mr Van Ellen. Seeing the police as his only hope, he had become patience itself, not even showing any irritation when Smith had to ask him several times how to spell out the foreign names.

So far, these people had proved even less helpful than those on Smith's other lists. Most were old school friends with whom the young Van Ellen had lost touch and the set whose dances, balls and coming-out parties he had attended a few years earlier. The message from all of them so far had tallied broadly with what the last young fop had expressed: 'Lost touch with the old boy when he dropped out and went all arty. Only did it to nark Papa if you ask me. I expect he'll grow out of it when Pater cuts him off.'

Having drawn a blank, Smith was itching to get back to the Van Ellen servants whom he felt sure knew more than they were telling, and to the boy's sister who, so far, was a bit of a mystery. He'd gained reluctant permission to question all of them again. Reluctant, partly because Van Ellen was not only certain that any information available in the household would already be known to him, but was also anxious for Smith to get to work, discreetly, elsewhere.

So Smith plodded on, but while having a think about it as he made his way from one mansion or town house to another, he hit upon a ruse. He would report back for the personal conferences for which Van Ellen seemed eager, but which, so far, he had resisted. Whilst there, he would bite off one or two of the household at a time, with the excuse of striking while the iron was hot, filling in details that might not have concerned the busy master of the household, and getting a fresh eye view. All the sort of things Best might have said.

He was not sure how Best would have coped with one added embarrassment – the attentions of Helen Franks, partly because the Sergeant's own reactions in that quarter seemed to fluctuate. Helen was badgering Smith to know how the enquiry was going. How far they had got? Best had made it clear that he no longer trusted her, so he told her nothing. The arrival of a letter from Best put paid to Smith's investigations and musings about Van Ellen. He dropped all the Van Ellen business for the time being and headed for City Road Basin.

Smith sat on a high stool at a desk in the offices of the Grand Junction Canal Company. He was setting about the latest task given him by Best. At least, he thought ruefully, he didn't have another list of people to chase around after. All he had to do, he reflected, as the office fire flickered away in the background, was to find out which boats would have been going south at Marsworth on the night of the murder and the names of the skippers. Once he had that, he would have a bit more chasing about to do, finding the skippers, if they were about, discovering if they knew Minchin, who their crews were, and if they were particular friends of Minchin.

The names of the crews were not registered, only that of the skipper who did his own hiring. Smith's task would be complicated by the fact that many people would have at least a passing aquaintance with Minchin through his job at City Road, but maybe that would also be a help as they might know who his friends were. He was cross-checking several registers handed to him by Albert Thornley's assistant, the traffic manager himself being on his day off.

A couple of hours later, he had before him a list of twelve fly boats, travelling in two groups of six, and several lone operators.

'If you go down there now you should catch one of the gangs getting ready to leave tonight,' the assistant told him. 'But they'll be working so you'll have to catch them when they are having a break.'

'This is a murder enquiry,' Smith informed him with all the dignity he could muster, 'so I think they must be prepared to break their routine, if necessary.'

The assistant looked startled at the young man's temerity. Maybe he was older than he looked and of higher rank? But Smith was not done. 'I think you should come down with me, point them out, and tell them they must co-operate with me. I will not detain them unnecessarily.' He stood back and raised his hand to allow the assistant through the door before him, carried out in a mild but determined manner which brooked no refusal without confrontation. Best would have been proud of him. Looking confused, the assistant complied.

'Does Mr Thornley always have Saturdays off?' he asked conversationally, as they made their way through the stacks of barrels and piles of boxes.

The assistant nodded. 'Always. I have Tuesday.'

'When does he come back?'

'Sunday afternoon.' The assistant looked puzzled.

'It's just helpful to know when he is available here, in case I have any more questions.'

'Of course.'

Minchin had gone missing on a Saturday night.

None of the boatmen, all of whom had been working on the night in question, had been particular friends of Minchin, or, if they were, they were not saying and neither were their colleagues. There seemed to be some resentment in their responses which puzzled the young constable. He decided to plunge straight in. 'Didn't you like him?' he asked the skipper of the *Viking*, a mild, sandy-haired man with pale-blue eyes and spiky eyelashes.

'Weren't that,' interrupted Headley, his second-in-command, a stumpy fellow with smallpox scars.

'Ain't no need to tell the constable that,' complained the skipper.

'No? Why not?' Headley straightened himself belligerently. 'It's our living, ain't it?'

Smith grasped what was going on. 'You don't like men from the wharves being put on the boats?'

'Would you? Would you fancy someone going around arresting people and saying they was policemen?'

Smith smiled and admitted he wouldn't.

'There's boatmen without work an' these idiots get to ride instead of 'em.'

'There weren't none down here when they needed them,' the skipper sighed, as though he had been through all this before, several times. 'It was only the once.'

'Twice. And the skippers should've refused. They have the say.'

'An' they need to keep their jobs!' shouted the skipper. 'Youse ought to be glad you got one!'

'Twice?' asked Smith.

'Yerse. They took on another. For a trip just ahead of ours.'
'An' it ran late!'

'One man wouldn't cause that.'

'Oh yes he did! He didn't—'

'Where was that?' Smith broke in, the technicalities were not important.

'I dunno,' said the skipper.

'I do,' said the truculent Headley. 'Top lock at Linslade, weren't it? Made them late for the rest of the trip, made us back up behind 'em.'

'Would that mean they would be late at Marsworth?' enquired the constable, trying to stop his pencil quivering over the page. His knowledge of the Grand Junction layout was sketchy, but his excitement was intense. He sensed he was on to something.

'Well, what do you think?' said Headley, as usual, answering a question with a question.

'I don't know,' said Smith gripping the pencil so that it made deep dents in his fingers.

' 'Course it did,' he answered. 'Just up the line from Maffers, innit?'

'I don't know,' repeated Smith.

'Well, it is,' put in the skipper. He glared at Headley.

Nearly choking with the effort to keep the question casual, Smith murmured, 'You don't . . . you don't happen to know who this man was, do you?'

'No, we doesn't,' said the skipper, politely but firmly.

'Don't us?' laughed Headley. ' 'Course us do! It was 'im, over there.'

He pointed over to where a darkly handsome, muscular man was loading bales of material on to an already heavily laden boat. As though alerted, the man glanced over. It was Sam Grealey.

Chapter Seventeen

Now that Smith possessed this riveting information he was at a loss how to use it. He could scarcely arrest Grealey for being at Marsworth on the same night as Minchin and, if he questioned the man, he might just alert him further. He might also ask all the wrong questions and prepare him for the right ones. In any case, he might have it all wrong. He recalled his misplaced euphoria over 'Mary Evans' which had led to his traipsing after the Minchin lad and his friend.

All of Smith's new-found confidence deserted him as he wrestled over the problem of whether to speak to Grealey and if so, what to say. If only Best were there. Or even Cheadle. None of the other Inspectors knew enough about the case to be of any help. He should, of course, go directly to Superintendent Williamson, head of the Detective Branch at the Yard, but he would have gone home now, and Best was due back in the morning. Only he knew everything that was going on.

Smith decided to wait, hoping desperately that his glance of interest had not alerted the suspect. He completed his chat to the crew of the *Viking* in a leisurely fashion, then began to stroll away without looking towards Grealey.

As he did so, it suddenly occurred to him that if he didn't speak to the man he definitely would be alerted. After all, he'd spoken to all the others who were on the fly boat string that night and asked them if they saw or knew

Minchin. Why would he leave out Grealey? He stopped, tapped his head and shook it in a manner which he hoped indicated to any onlooker that he had almost forgotten to do something but suddenly remembered, then wandered across to where Grealey was working.

He summoned up all his newly acquired acting skills and approached Grealey with his hand outstretched and a friendly smile upon his face.

'Hello, there. Remember me? Constable Smith. Saw you with Mr Thornley at the Yard. 'Course, you know our Mr Best quite well . . . '

Grealey's guarded look softened a little. 'Oh aye, we're mates.'

'He told me,' Smith grinned. 'Been through a bit of business together by all accounts.'

That evidently pleased the man. 'We have, we have. Saw him up at the inquest yesterday s'matter of fact.'

'Oh, is that so.' Smith nodded. 'Well, I've come down here to talk to some of the men who were on the canal the night Minchin went missing. But I expect Mr Best already asked you about that.'

Grealey hesitated. Smith was willing to bet that Best didn't know he was at Marsworth that night. 'Oh, yeah.' He rubbed his grimy hands together then wiped them on his trousers in a vain attempt to dispose of some of the dirt. 'Bad business that. Bad business.'

Smith nodded. 'Yes, terrible.'

'Was they any help?' He nodded towards the boatmen.

Smith spread his hands and shrugged. 'No, not really. They didn't see him or anything. Or, if they did, they can't remember.'

'One night's much like another on the canal.'

'I expect so – on the beat as well!'

They both chuckled at that.

'She threw a spanner in the works, his missus y'know.'

'So I hear! Funny business, isn't it?' He paused. 'So you don't remember seeing Minchin that night either?'

Another slight hesitation. This wasn't going right. He would be alerted. 'S'matter of fact I did see him,' Grealey replied eventually. 'Just for a minute, in passing, you know.' Clever move that – tell us what we might already know. 'But we was late; I expect they told you about that,' he grimaced. 'My fault.'

Smith laughed. 'We've all got to learn.'

'Right, but I don't think they' – he nodded towards the fly-boat crews – 'saw it that way.'

'Oh well, I expect they were frightened you might be taking their jobs.'

'Not much chance of that.'

'Anyway, he seemed all right, did he? Minchin?'

'Oh yeah, for him, you know. Always a bit of a misery but, matter of fact, he was more matey than usual. Felt out of it a bit, same as me, I reckon.'

'Didn't say anything which might indicate. . . ?'

'Nuffink, nuffink. I was as amazed as the next man.'

'Bit chippy was he?'

'No, as I says, seemed all right to me.'

'You didn't see anyone following him into the trees?'

Grealey shook his head. 'No, like I said, we was only jawing for half a crack, we was busy.'

'Fair enough,' said Smith casually, then held up a warning finger. 'Mr Best might want another word with you – just for the record you understand.' He did his best to make it sound of little importance.

'Anything I can do, just say,' said Grealey piously. 'That poor woman.' He shook his head, ' 'Ow he could do that, I dunno.'

As far as Smith could tell the man seemed unperturbed. 'Right, thanks,' he said, patting the loader's arm and turning to go. As he did so, Grealey took a sudden step forward, put his hand out to halt the constable and exclaimed, 'They think . . . ' Then he recovered himself enough to lower his voice and mutter conversationally, 'They think he just topped himself then, do they?'

'Between you and me,' Smith confided, 'that's what it looks like.'

'Yeah, I thought so.'

'But we've got to make enquiries. You know how it is.'

'Oh, I does, I does.' He returned the farewell salute of his new-found friend and went back to his work.

PC Smith sat in Mrs Minchin's shabby front room drinking tea from an unmatching cup and saucer and watching the lady finish her ironing. She did it quite well. Not as well as his mother, of course. Not so organized. But she looked pretty doing it and the new little jet brooch at her neck sparkled in the firelight as she moved.

Indeed, he was surprised at how much better she looked since her husband's death, despite the fact she had been so worried about him when he last saw her. The room was brighter, too; indeed there was a vase of golden chrysanthemums on what passed as a sideboard and a lady's magazine on the rickety table. How had she managed to afford those? Wasn't she supposed to be penniless? He shrugged, maybe the company had sent them – or a friend. That's what it must be. A friend had brought them to cheer her up.

He was not there to see Mrs Minchin, he reminded himself, but young George. While he was down at the City Road Basin he thought he might as well pop in to see how the lad was getting on with his drawing. Despite the wild goose chase, he liked the little fellow. Being from a large family himself he was used to having kids around and missed them now he lived in the section house.

But George was out playing. Mrs Minchin knew not where but said he should be in shortly, what with evening coming on, his supper waiting to be demolished, and having that new toy fort to play with. So his namesake had a cup of tea which he would have been churlish to refuse, and chatted to Mrs Minchin while he waited.

The time passed surprisingly quickly. Mrs Minchin regaled him with stories of her trip to Marsworth which, since she had never been north of the Holloway Road before, had obviously been a great adventure for her. And one she related with a certain mischievous humour, too, particularly when it came to describing the ministrations of a certain Mr Cheadle.

Her picture of the Chief Inspector was one Smith had the greatest difficulty in recognizing, so he presumed she must be exaggerating wildly – but nonetheless to great effect. He watched, transfixed by the way she raised her eyebrows and widened her eyes in wonder as she recalled all the sights she had seen, and even laughed once or twice. No doubt, there was something about the woman. Occasionally, a catch in her voice or a mistiness of her eye indicated an underlying sadness. Maybe she cried on her own at night. That's what his mother had done. Maybe she didn't really care?

'Sam Grealey saw your husband on the canal that night,' he said suddenly, then was immediately sorry. Her face whitened instantly and all joy drained from it.

She went on ironing and whispered, 'He never said.'

'Maybe he didn't want to upset you.'

She gave him a look which suggested that the thought of Sam Grealey being sensitive was an alien one. Interesting in itself, thought Smith.

She frowned. 'Why was he on the canal?'

'Helping out, like your husband,' he said kindly, trying to get back to the previous intimacy, 'but he was on his way down, not up.'

'What did he say?'

'Oh, nothing much. Nothing of any use anyway. Just saw him in passing.' He paused, then said, 'He didn't notice anything wrong.'

There were no more tantalizing tales of the trip to Marsworth. She was lost now in her ironing and her thoughts. He would have given a lot to know what these were. Somehow he felt they were important. He was about to press her further when a sharp knock at the door brought them both back to reality. Mrs Minchin went over to the window, peered out through the curtains, turned with a puzzled look and, flatteringly, beckoned Smith to share the view and perhaps solve the mystery. Standing so close to her waiflike body made Smith feel immensely tall, protective, very masculine, and quite excited. The vision which met his eyes through the window quickly deflated him. It was that awful female, Helen Franks.

Miss Franks, it appeared, had come to see Mrs Minchin merely to express her condolences. Smith thought it much more likely that she had come to discover what was happening, how much Mrs Minchin knew, and whether, in fact, it was likely that Mrs Minchin's husband had killed her sister. He couldn't tell her they had a possible identification of the victim in case it raised her hopes, but managed her easy removal from the Minchin household with the hint that he did have some news. His mind was a morass of confusion as to what it would be all right for her to know and what it would not, but he decided that a quick résumé of his inquiries about Minchin's movements on the night would not harm, and the doubt about his suicide might divert her sufficiently to stop her hounding Mrs Minchin.

Carried away by his tale and made careless by tiredness, he also allowed Sam Grealey's sighting of Minchin to creep into the story before sensing he had said too much.

Realizing his error, he followed it up quickly with another titbit and breathed a sigh that, with luck, she had not noticed. He was wrong.

He left her waiting for an omnibus home but as soon as he turned the corner she walked away from the stop – towards City Road Basin. Helen Franks was sick and tired of all this shilly-shallying, she wanted to know what was going on and she sensed that Sam Grealey might be just the one to tell her.

The Great Hall at Euston Railway Station was one of the grandest places Constable Smith had ever seen. It was not his first visit, he had been there many times before, but its Romanesque columns and marble staircases never failed to impress him. This, and the hustle and bustle of railway travel always excited him. Such a mix of people – from the grandest, first-class travellers surrounded by scurrying servants, fussily shepherding hampers and elegant leather portmanteaux – to the pathetically poor, with their cloth bundles and anxious expressions. Smith was here to meet one particular, second-class passenger carrying one small carpet bag.

He would have been happy to have lingered but Sergeant Ernest Best was due in any minute, so he hurried past the statue of George Stephenson on through to the arrival platform in the more workaday, but still impressive, train shed. His Sergeant had decided his aims would be better served by returning to London that night, instead of the following day as scheduled, much to Smith's relief. He was pleased he had decided to pop into the Yard in the hope of catching a senior officer to consult, and had spied Best's telegraph instead.

When Helen spied the Grand Junction wharf gate, she realized that to gain entry she must either demand to see

Mr Thornley, whom she had met at the Regent's Park explosion inquest, or adopt a humbler pose and sneak in among the lorries, carts and wagons and canal folk toing and froing through them. But Albert Thornley might not be there. What then? In any case, making it formal was not what she wanted. She would not get much from Grealey under the watchful eye of his boss.

Drawing her grey shawl more tightly over her black coat, she lowered her head and opted for the humble. Thank goodness she limited bright colours to her artist's palette. Her sombre dress had not been arrived at accidentally or through any personal tastes. She dressed thus because she had discovered that an unremarkable appearance served an independent-minded woman best, by limiting her visibility. The strategy stood her in good stead once again. She waited until a brace of carts and a group of people were entering and mingled with them while the gate-keeper was distracted. She was in. Now what?

Tired, cold and dirty from his journey though he was, Best felt pleased and excited about what Smith had learned of Grealey and confirmed that the man had not told him he had been on the canal that night. It followed he must have something to hide.

Grealey and Thornley kept popping up in this drama like rabbits out of a magician's hat. This time, he must not let his quarry go but, like Smith, he was at first unsure how to proceed. His first instincts were to rush down to City Road Basin and beard the pair in their den. But where was the evidence? It was that pair who had put them on Minchin's trail and Grealey had been on the canal that night and been seen talking to Minchin but had not told them. Grealey was a one for the ladies but that was no crime. It could be a motive though.

Mary Elizabeth had made regular visits to the wharves to deliver and collect her post. Grealey could have made her acquaintance then. A lovers' tiff? Had she had become a burden? Had she repelled his advances? The oldest and the commonest motives were the most likely, as Cheadle would doubtless have lectured them.

But where did Albert Thornley fit in? Had both been involved with the woman? Unlikely when she had lost her previous employment through her objections to the advances of her employer. Couldn't quite see the ever-anxious Albert Thornley in that light, either, but maybe he was anxious for a reason other than the company's problems.

'I need time to think,' Best told the eagerly awaiting Smith. He also wanted to see Helen Franks, so when Smith began burbling on about their meeting and how he thought they should tell her the victim was not her sister as soon as possible he made a sudden decision. He hailed a cab and directed him to the Holland Park address. He could do his thinking *en route* – if Smith would just shut up for a minute.

Helen was passed on towards her quarry by several puzzled workmen, too busy and preoccupied to allow their puzzlement to develop further. She found Sam Grealey guiding a sack of sugar from a hoist into a fly boat. It seemed obvious by his agitated concentration and bad-tempered reactions to the hoist operator's placings that he was trying to hurry the task and making mistakes in the process. She waited until he had the sack stowed and was watching for the next one before calling out to him. He glanced at her with puzzlement and irritation.

'Mr Grealey?'

'Yeah,' he grunted, his arms already extended, awaiting their next burden.

'Can I talk to you?'

'What about?'

'It's a private matter.'

He had the next sack in his arms and was frowning at it, 'Aren't you the sister of . . . of that missing girl?'

'Yes, Matilda Franks. It's about her.'

That got his full attention. He stared at her. 'I don't know nothing about her! Why should I know anything about her?'

'I'm not saying you do. I . . . I'd just like some advice.' This was hopeless.

Grealey turned his back to bed down another sack bound for Leicester then turned. 'Don't know what I can tell you. Anyways, I'm behind here, can't stop.' He was panting a little.

'Oh, please . . . help me . . . '

'You'll have to wait until I've finished. This here's due out in an hour.' He looked around the side of the wooden crate now in his grasp, 'Go and sit over there among them boxes,' he ordered, indicating a spot against the warehouse wall before returning to his task. He looked tense. 'But you're wastin' your time,' he called after her, then muttered to himself, 'What the 'ell's goin' on?'

Chapter Eighteen

Grealey showed no sign of being finished yet and the night air was getting distinctly chilly. Helen was certain she had already been sitting for much more than an hour, trying to look inconspicuous, against the wall of the warehouse.

Looking inconspicuous became more difficult as work on other craft ceased and the men drifted away out of the gates or set off in the boats. Grealey had been telling the truth. He was well behind with his loading. The last, in fact. But although this thinning out at first caused her to become more conspicuous, eventually her small figure was almost lost in the shadows as the many lights were dowsed or dwindled away when boats left.

They disappeared even more quickly as fog began to descend, settle, and thicken about her.

Coming here had been a mistake; she realized that now. Her vigil had given her time to mull over what she was going to ask Grealey, but rather than clarifying her thoughts they had become more confused. What did she expect to get from him? *If that Sergeant Best had done his job properly*, she thought bitterly, *this action would not have been necessary*. Nevertheless, she began to wish he was here with his certainties, his cheerful demeanour, his shiny boots and his warm brown eyes.

Mrs Briggs's usually equable and sensible demeanour had deserted her and been replaced by agitation.

'Miss Helen's not here!' she exclaimed, when Best asked to see her mistress. 'She hasn't come home!'

Best's hand trembled slightly as he reached into his vest pocket for his half-hunter. It was after midnight, 12.45 a.m., in fact. 'She must have been held up somewhere.'

'No, no. She would have told me. She knows how much I worry, particularly since Matilda went missing.' Her eyes widened as the thought suddenly bore in on her that Helen, too, might not return. She put her hand over her mouth as though stopping further words would prevent the dreadful reality.

'But people don't always *know* when they might be late.'

Mrs Briggs shushed him with a gesture. 'She's never this late! Never.'

Best patted her hand. 'The fog must have held her up. It did us. The cabbie got lost.' He paused, 'Now, did she say where she was going?'

She looked uncertain, then embarrassed, 'Oh, I might as well tell you,' she shrugged. 'She was going to see Mrs Minchin.'

He quelled Smith with a sharp glance. 'I see. Well, that's a long way, and it does get very foggy down there, near the canal. We'll wait a little while.' He smiled gently. 'We would love a cup of tea.'

'Oh, of course, of course.' She brushed vainly at her wet eyes. 'I'm so glad you are here. I didn't know what to do.'

'You told me she was on her way home when you left her!' he accused Smith, as soon as the housekeeper was out of earshot.

'She was, Sergeant, she was. I left her at the omnibus stop.'

'But you didn't wait to see her get on?'

'No. She said she was perfectly all right and just told me to go – that she wasn't a baby and it was insulting to a woman to be treated like one.'

That sounded like Helen.

Best knew his concern was probably out of proportion. The woman was an adult and a damned difficult one. But, he discerned, Smith's guilty demeanour was somewhat out of proportion as well. His eyes narrowed and he looked directly at his colleague. Then, placing great emphasis on every word, he said slowly, 'There is something you haven't told me.'

Smith was no tight-lipped villain with wits honed by experience to resist the Sergeant's accusations. Indeed, it was the lad's very openness that had landed him in this situation. 'I didn't mean to,' he protested, 'I mean, I know I shouldn't have,' Smith pleaded, 'it just sort of slipped out . . . '

'What did!' hissed Best. 'Tell me what!'

'I told her what I'd found out about Grealey.'

At last Grealey was finished. Now, he stood before Helen, wiping his hands down the sides of his trousers, his expression hostile and suspicious. 'Well,' he grated, 'what d'you want with me, then?' He had taken her around the side of the warehouse while he collected his belongings.

'I just hoped you might be able to help me regarding my sister . . . ' The true foolishness of her action had sunk in as she realized how quiet, dark and deserted the wharf had become. She must not show her fear. There must at least be a nightwatchman about. She tried to look Grealey in the eye, but her eyes kept straying to his bulging biceps which he was flexing and unflexing.

'Why should I know your sister?' he snapped, not making the least attempt to be polite.

Helen bristled. 'I think you might just hear me out.'

'Why should I? What are you to me?' His eyes were angry and hard, 'Just another bloody interfering, difficult woman.' He turned his back and began to walk off.

She must stop him going, 'I know you knew her!' she shouted, wildly. 'I have evidence that you knew her.'

He stopped sharply in his tracks then turned slowly to look at her. 'Don't talk rubbish, woman!' he yelled. 'She was no sister of yours. Your sister would be posh . . . '

The silence grew thunderous as the portent of what he had just said struck home to both of them. Helen froze as Grealey stepped menacingly towards her.

The dense fog not only provided a possible reason for the non-arrival of Helen, it greatly hampered Best and Smith as they tried to find a cab to take them down to the City Road Basin. The ranks were empty. The few vehicles stumbling along the roads were either carrying passengers already, their anxious faces peering around the hoods trying to assist in the wearisome business of identifying their whereabouts, or were driven by cabbies bent only on finding their own way home.

Typical, thought Best. They jam our streets when it's fine and desert us when we need them most. Finally, he resorted to extreme, life-threatening measures. When the next unoccupied growler happened along he jumped out into the road in front of it, arms held aloft in the approved police fashion and blowing a whistle at the same time. The cabbie, who saw him only at the last minute, was forced to bring his horse to a rearing, shuddering halt.

'You stupid bastard!' he yelled. 'You could have killed us both!'

The worst of his subsequent oaths grudgingly faded when Best displayed his warrant card, declared that they were on police business, and demanded he take them to Bertrand's house in Notting Hill, and then, if necessary, to the City Road Basin. Cabbies depended on the police for their licences and swearing was an offence for which they could be banned.

In such a pea-souper, the cabbie needed all the help he could get. Smith took the first turn carrying the flare aloft.

At first he walked several yards ahead but soon had to close the gap when the fog grew even thicker and their crawl slowed down almost to a stumbling halt in that soundless world. The sulphurous, sooty air was almost suffocating, reaching into their mouths and noses and making their eyes weep.

They began to move a little faster once they reached the wider, better lit Uxbridge Road where light from the odd flare approaching from the other direction also helped them keep to their own side of the road.

When Grealey stepped towards her so menacingly, Helen didn't hesitate. She turned and ran – straight into the blackness of the tall warehouse which loomed behind her. At first, she fled wildly and blindly into the void but, as her eyes adjusted, she could see that she was in a wide central aisle. Towers of crates, boxes and barrels rose on both sides. She dodged down one of the side paths leading from the aisle and stood quite still, trying to get her breath and quieten her pounding heart.

Grealey had been less lucky in his progress. She had heard metallic crashing noises behind her back, near the entrance to the warehouse, then the tinkle of breaking glass and Grealey's furious curses. These had now ceased, to be replaced by angry mutterings, the faint rasp of matches being struck followed by brief flickerings of light and odd tinkling and scraping sounds. Then, more curses as the matches spluttered out and fingers were burned.

Suddenly, a cold hand clutched at her stomach. She realized what the noises were and just what Grealey was doing. He must have fallen over some lanterns near the entrance. Now he was trying to find one ready for use. Once he did so and it flared into life it would only be a matter of time, a very short space of time, before he found her. He need only wander down the central aisle swinging his light from right to left and there she would be – revealed, trapped, cowering beneath a stack of boxes, utterly defenceless. She must move!

Once through Notting Hill, Best took the flare. He was more likely to recognize the side street which led to Bertrand's house. That was the theory. But the fog had grown denser again. The earlier ghostly railings of Hyde Park, with their gated landmarks, had now disappeared altogether. Without them, it was impossible to gauge where they were. Also gone were the dim shapes of the tall mansions to his left and any other traffic. They were in a blank tunnel.

Best was too distracted and frantic to notice what the horse manure was doing to his boots. Neither would he have cared. A fear was growing in him that made him want to cry out. Since Emma had died in his arms, he had never allowed himself to become so concerned about another person. Now, he felt the same despair of not being able to do anything to help the woman he knew he really cared for. And it was his fault! He should have seen to it that she was informed that Matilda was not the victim instead of waiting to tell her himself. What would he do if he was too late to save her! The tears blurring his vision were not entirely due to the stinging murk around him. Abruptly, the fog thinned enough for him to recognize the turnings. It was an omen!

When they reached Bertrand's house, Best felt another surge of hope. Even in the yellow-grey gloom it was visible. Not only was it lit throughout, there was noisy talk and even shouts of laughter coming from within. At this time of night! Helen was there! That could be the only explanation.

Helen took off her shoes and began edging towards the side of the building, in the hope that she might reach a pathway parallel to the central aisle. Then she could hide behind a stack and, as Grealey passed, make her way back towards the entrance. If she didn't, if this pathway were a dead end – she was done for. She sidled very slowly and quietly until the next match was struck then, under the cover of the noise Grealey was making with the lanterns, she moved faster. Grit from the floor dug into her feet and splinters from the rough wooden crates bit into her face and fingers. All at once, a wider and brighter light radiated down the central aisle and a shout of satisfaction echoed through the building. Grealey had lit his lantern and was coming for her.

It was an exuberant and excited Jacques Bertrand who opened the door to greet Best and Smith. 'Come in, come in,' he beckoned, as though it were the most normal thing in the world for two policemen to come calling in a dense fog well after midnight.

'You will not believe who is here!' he exclaimed jubilantly. 'You just will not believe it. It is astonishing!' He led his grimy and confused guests into his front parlour then stood back and extended his right arm with a flourish. Best's heart sank. There stood a young man and woman.

The woman was not Helen.

As he struggled to control his disappointment, he realized he recognized her companion. It was the baby-faced young man he had seen only once before, briefly, at the meeting of the Regent's Canal Disaster Committee. It was Eddie Van Ellen, the budding artist. The exquisitely pretty young woman also seemed vaguely familiar.

'Matilda!' announced Bertrand pushing her forward with great glee. 'She is found.'

Best sat down with a thump. 'So I see,' he said, tonelessly. 'So I see.'

'Wait till we tell Helen!' continued a euphoric Bertrand. 'If only we could go to Holland Park right now,' – he peered out of the window – 'but it does not look possible ...'

'We could only get this far ...' explained a smiling Matilda.

'She's not there,' interrupted Best bluntly.

Matilda was the first to sense that all was not well. 'What do you mean?' she asked nervously. 'Where is she?'

'We don't know. She's missing.' He looked at this pretty, happy young woman in the ice-blue silk gown, and felt the urge to hurt her. 'She went looking for you,' he said coldly, 'and now she's gone. She may be in great danger.'

He had intended to disturb her, but even Best was startled by the way Matilda's face instantly crumpled like that of a child from whom a favourite toy has been seized. A cry of utmost anguish issued from her throat.

There was no point in trying to hide her movements now. Helen knew she must move fast. Her left foot came down on something sharp and pointed and she managed only to half-stifle the cry of pain before hobbling on frantically. The swinging light of Grealey's lantern grew brighter – then dimmed again as he inspected each side track. But always growing brighter. Soon it would be illuminating her. She *must* go faster.

The impact almost knocked her out. Her left side had crashed into something extremely solid. Desperately she felt upwards, to the sides and all around. There was no break in it. It was the warehouse wall. There was no gap in the stacks of merchandise on either side before her. That meant there was no pathway alongside the wall. That meant she was trapped.

Thank goodness the waiting cab was a four-wheeler so there was room enough for Matilda, Van Ellen and

Bertrand, who insisted on joining in the hunt for Helen. Best usually hated having 'civvies' along, with their unreliable reactions. But he might learn something from them as to where else Helen might have gone and there were more pairs of hands for carrying extra flares.

They were back on the Uxbridge Road heading for Marble Arch when Smith voiced a thought which had already occurred to Best, but been dismissed, 'Shouldn't we try to find a police station and send an electric telegraph to the police station closest to City Road?'

Best shook his head, gesturing towards the enveloping fog which had closed in even more tightly. 'Look, it's getting worse. Notting Hill station is back there, the next is Marylebone, and if we get off the main road again, what chance have we of finding it again quickly – never mind the police station? Then we would waste time explaining and writing the telegraph and there may not be a line clear . . . ' He shook his head. 'We'll be better off sticking to the main roads and going as fast as we can.'

He wished he was as sure as he sounded. He handed his flare to the young Van Ellen, admonished the driver to get a move on, and weighed into a tearful Matilda and an agitated Bertrand.

He learned of other places where Helen might have gone. Alas none of them very near nor very likely. He also learned that Eddie and Matilda had eloped to Gretna Green, then stayed in Scotland while Eddie painted Matilda in the Highlands, both unaware of the furore they were causing. She had told Mrs Briggs that she was going to Pinner for a long stay and couldn't understand why she became worried. Best thought this was not the time to tell her that their housekeeper didn't always listen carefully to her employers. Once married, Matilda had written to Helen in Paris but by then she must have left. Bertrand's closeness with Helen was also explained when, in the course of conversation, he had shrugged and said simply, 'She is my cousin.' Best wanted to cry.

Helen struggled to overcome her panic and began to feel around the crate in front of her. Maybe there was a way onto the top of the stack. The light, only two stacks away now, briefly lit what should have been the next crate up but she could see nothing. Grealey's mutterings became louder.

She pulled herself up to the first side strut and felt for the top of the crate. It stood proud, forming a ledge! A wide ledge. She blessed all that childhood tree-climbing and the lugging around of huge canvases which had strengthened her arms.

She gathered all her strength to haul herself upwards again. Her elbows were on the top of the crate, another haul would do it. Would she have the strength? Damn these skirts, tangling around her legs and adding such weight to her body. She pushed herself up, expecting at any moment to come up against the next crate in the stack. But so far, there was none. Now she was leaning forward half on and half off the crate, panting and exhausted, without the strength for the final heave. A burst of light all around her made her realize that it must be over, she was done for. She awaited her fate.

Miraculously, the light faded again with retreating footsteps. Grealey was in the path behind her – the light had come through the sides of the stack. She still had a chance. The knowledge gave her the necessary strength. She heaved herself onto the top of the crate. Once there, the intermittent flashes of light revealed what she had hoped for all along. There *was* a path ahead. It had been blocked only by the crate she was now on.

She turned around and began lowering herself down the other side – feeling for the first strut with her toes, found it then lowered her right leg in search of the second strut. But her fingers began to lose their grip, her right leg was swinging about – destroying her balance. To save herself she tried to jump, but tumbled awkwardly and noisily onto the hard ground, her foot twisting beneath her.

There was a yell of triumph from among the merchandise stacks to her right, 'Oh, so there you are my beauty!'

Grealey was running towards her, the light jumping about like approaching flames from hell. Helen scrambled to her feet, crying out with pain from her right ankle as she did so. She tried to move forward but her skirt was caught. She ripped away at the waist fastenings, got free as Grealey entered the pathway out of which she had climbed! She ran forward blindly. She might still escape. Then something solid, very solid, smashed into her face and she fell into a deep, deep void.

They were making better progress along Oxford Street, where the lighting was more abundant. But not enough for Best. 'For God's sake man, hurry!' he shouted at the driver. 'You must go faster!' The man was trying his best, caught up as he now was in the urgency of their quest. But abandoned vehicles kept looming into his path causing the horses to rear in fright and veer into the pavement.

At last they were at Tottenham Court Road where they turned north. Best wasn't sure it was the most direct route but probably the simplest.

Grealey, made gargoyle-like by the lantern on the floor beneath him, stood over a crumpled Helen and complained aggressively, 'Why did you run like that you stupid woman! I told you I wouldn't hurt you, didn't I? What d'you think I am?' He laughed and reached down towards her, removing his filthy neckerchief with his other hand as he did so. She tried to twist away but came up against the warehouse wall. 'Don't be so stupid!' he exclaimed angrily. 'You can't get away!'

She must be seeing double. Looming above Grealey was another, taller figure, holding something aloft.

'Thank God!' she cried. 'Oh, thank God!' She gasped with relief – just as the club in the traffic manager's hand smashed down on Sam Grealey's skull.

They had reached the City Road when one of the horses stumbled into an abandoned cartwheel and became lame, slowing down the carriage even more. But it made no difference. Best was now running ahead, sobbing as he ran, knowing in his heart he must be too late. He had not been able to save the first woman he loved, why should he be able to save this one?

A wiry but strong hand was pushing Helen's face down towards the water.

'You were stupid to come here,' snarled Thornley, 'very, very stupid. You don't know your way around and, in the dark, you stumbled into the water and drowned – running away from Grealey.' His grip on her head tightened. Helen struggled against his forcing hand, but it was useless. He gave a final push and her face hit the filthy, evil-smelling water and went beneath. Now, the water was her eyes, her mouth, her nose. Choking, gurgling, she still struggled, fighting desperately for her life. As her world again descended into darkness she wondered why dying had to be so noisy – all that shouting – and why was she being pulled and shaken about so much? Wasn't it supposed to be peaceful?

Chapter Nineteen

It was peaceful now. Deathly quiet in fact. Slowly, Helen ventured to open her eyes just a little, then promptly shut them again. The light increased the thudding pain radiating from the back of her head.

After a while, she tried again. When they were almost fully open a man's hand came into view – it was coming towards her! She screamed.

The hand grasped hers. 'It's all right, it's all right, it's only me.' She squinted dazedly into Best's warm, greeny-grey eyes. 'You're safe. You're at home in bed now.' He carried her hand up to his cheek. 'I won't let anything happen to you ever again.'

As the mental mists cleared she became angry. 'Where were you?' she complained, unreasoningly.

'Trying to reach you as quickly as we could.'

'We?'

He hesitated, looking up to the other side of the bed. 'There is someone here to see you.'

A smiling Matilda swam into Helen's view. She cried out again but, this time, with sheer joy.

'She taunted me,' claimed Thornley. 'She led me on and then pushed me away and taunted me.'

'I don't think so,' said Best, to whom this excuse was very old. He thought it particularly unlikely to be true on this occasion. 'I think you wanted her, a pretty, young girl, and she didn't want you. It was as simple as that.'

Even in the cause of extracting a confession, Best felt in no mood to humour the man who had just tried to murder Helen.

'It was an accident. I was angry at something she said and I just gave her a push.'

Best shook his head. 'No, I don't think so.'

'It's my word against hers.'

The man was unbelievable. 'We caught you, remember! And what about Grealey?'

'He was attacking her.'

'Oh, I see, you saved her. How gallant.' Thornley tried to interrupt, but Best was really angry now. 'And then there's poor bloody Minchin! What had that man ever done to you?'

The traffic manager fell silent.

'I'll tell you what he did: he provided you with a useful scapegoat. You guessed he was under suspicion when we asked where he was. What better solution than to kill him and make it seem like a guilty suicide.'

Thornley's lip curled. 'Don't be stupid. How could it be me, way up there?'

Best realized he was losing it. He should be making friends with the man, letting all the things he had done seem reasonable and understandable. Making him feel like *he* was the victim. But he just couldn't.

'Easily, it was your night off. The train got you there ahead of them . . . ' He had no proof of this. No wonder the man was looking implacable. Never mind Best thought to himself, I've got him anyway for the murder of Mary Elizabeth and the attempted murder of Helen and Grealey. But he might just get away with manslaughter for Mary Elizabeth.

'We can prove you were there,' he exclaimed suddenly. 'You weren't as careful as you think.'

The silence hung between the handsome Best and this gaunt and unattractive middle-aged man. Best knew that some murderers had confessed merely because they had the irresistible urge to put the police right, prove they were more clever. The silence grew. *Ask me*, thought Best. *Ask me!* If he did, he had him.

'I dunno what you're talking about.'

Halfway there.

'You're talking rubbish.'

'I've got to admit that you were impressive. Nearly fooled us. Took some clever planning that.'

Was he mistaken. Did the man sit up a bit straighter, prouder?

'Want to know what gave you away?'

The man refused to meet his eyes.

'No? All right then.'

The tension had built up, Best allowed it to simmer a little longer, then he jumped in. 'It was those boots. We got the imprint.'

The man breathed out and sneered, 'Well, that's where you're wrong. I wasn't wearing these boots that night. You got it all wrong.'

'Put me right then,' said Best quietly.

'He was anxious I should know that he *didn't* poison Minchin. Didn't need to, he is stronger than he looks, he said. Thought we made it seem as if he took an unfair advantage.'

Even the wily Cheadle shook his head at this. Smith looked amazed. 'But . . . '

'He just waited in the bushes knowing that at some time Minchin would come in to pass water. All the men do somewhere there.'

'So he put Mary Elizabeth's body on the *Tilbury*?' asked Smith.

'Right. Did it in a panic just after he killed her. Thought that once it had got right to Braunston and was unloaded along with the other stuff it would be so much harder to prove where it had come from. The row at the lock and the writing on the wall were all part of a diversion.'

Smith held up a finger. ''Course, it was him that told us about the row. But why did he attack Helen?'

'He overheard her shouting to Grealey about having some evidence and he panicked again. The man was right out of his depth, you know.'

Cheadle leaned forward, hands on knees. He was still wreathed in the uncharacteristic amiability which disconcerted Best. 'What we needs to do,' he said earnestly, 'is try to keep all that about Minchin's other woman out of it. No sense in upsetting Betsy.'

'There wasn't another woman,' said Smith.

Both men turned to look at him.

'She did the scratches,' said the young man, 'Betsy did.' He blushed but carried on, 'They had a row about his gambling.'

It was Best's turn to be at a loss. 'But Grealey said . . . '

'They made it up about a girl friend so she wouldn't be embarrassed.' He too grew earnest. 'What we have to do is keep from Betsy that it was the scratches what made us suspicious and so caused his death.'

Best looked from one to another. A grizzled old Chief Inspector of many hard years' service and a youngster with promotion to lose – both willing to risk their careers by concealing evidence for the sake of little Mrs Minchin. But he knew they were fooling themselves: it would come out anyway. Mrs Minchin would be comforted – by whom? He thought he knew and this made him harbour a feeling he would not have previously credited: sympathy for Cheadle. But did the smitten young Smith realize what he might be doing to his chances of becoming a Scotland Yard detective?

In the event, Smith took this intelligence remarkably cheerfully. Due to his good work on the case, he had already been made Sergeant in charge of his division's local detectives, so felt able to bide his time. He was young enough and Cheadle would be retiring soon.

Helen's anger returned with a vengeance when she realized that Best already knew that the body in the canal was not that of her sister.

'You could have saved me some anguish – and that terrible time down at the wharf. It was all your fault!'

'I was going to tell you as soon as I got to London. Anyway,' he regrouped, 'if you hadn't been so difficult, concealing things and behaving so wilfully, I would never have been suspicious of you!' Although now besotted, Best had already grasped that the only way he could succeed with this lady was by fighting back.

'You *believed* I might have murdered my own sister!' she exclaimed. 'How *could* you?'

'It's been done,' he answered blithely. He couldn't stop smiling. 'Our first lovers' quarrel,' he grinned.

'Are you mad!' Helen yelled, then held her head and groaned, 'Oh, it hurts.'

'Oh, darling, I'm sorry.' He stroked her head gently which, she had to admit, was a soothing and very pleasant feeling. 'You know how I feel about you,' he said more softly, adding simply, 'I love you.'

She looked at him sadly and shook her head. 'It's no use, you know.'

'Why, for heaven's sake!'

'For the reasons I gave you on that walk to Bertrand's all that time ago.'

'But I wouldn't stop you painting, I'd love it.'

She shook her head again. 'And what if we had children?' She didn't wait for an answer. 'No,' she sighed, gazing at him with a certain longing, but speaking with a gathering determination. 'I would like to, but I just can't. Please don't persist.'

Best contemplated her sadly, then, to her apparent surprise and possibly some disappointment, he sat back and said quite amiably, 'Very well, I can't force you.'

'No.'

'But we can still be friends?'

'Of course.'

'And,' he hesitated, 'will you teach me how to paint?'

She looked at his handsome, eager face, laughed out loud and patted his hand. 'Of course I will, of course. I'd love to.'

That was all right then, he thought to himself. First stage of his strategy accomplished. Once on the scent, Ernest Best was relentless in pursuit.

Visit our website and discover thousands of other
History Press books.

www.thehistorypress.co.uk